UNHINGED

A DARK CAPTIVE CARTEL ROMANCE

ONCE UPON A VILLAIN

BIANCA COLE

UNHINGED PLAYLIST

'I Want It All'—Cameron Gray

'Talk Dirty'—Daniel Di Angelo

'Freak'—Lana Del Ray

'Waiting Game'—BANKS

'Lonely'—Azee

'Inside My Love'—Delilah

'Watch Me Burn'—Michele Morrone

'Taking Responsibility'—Kilo Kish

'Promises'—EMO

'Don't You Know'—Jaymes Young

'Blood In The Cut'—K.Flay, Aire Atlantica

'Till Death Do Us Part'—Rosenfeld

Listen on Spotify

DEDICATION

To Nicola Dooley who gave me the inspiration to write a mafia retelling of Alice falling for the Mad Hatter, thank you xx

AUTHOR'S NOTE

Hello reader,

This is a warning to let you know that this book is a **dark** mafia romance much like many of my other books, which means there are some sensitive subject matters addressed. If you've got any triggers, it would be a good idea to proceed with caution.

As well as a mad and possessive anti-hero, this book addresses some sensitive subjects. A full list of these can be found here. As always, this book has a HEA and there's no cheating.

If you have any triggers, then it's best to read the warnings and not proceed if any could be triggering for you. However, if none of these are an issue for you, read on and enjoy!

1

TAREN

*D*ark, soulless eyes dart across the courtyard as her soldiers await her command. There's a tension in the air that feels like it's stifling the oxygen in the room. It's always the same at cartel meetings like this. When her soldiers are here, it means she wants blood.

She opens her mouth, and everyone holds their breath collectively. "Bring me their blood in barrels." She paces in front of them. "By the time you return, I don't want any of the Guerra gang breathing, not even their families."

A shiver skates down my spine. There's a reason we call Ileana the Red Queen. And it's not because it's her favorite color. It's because she's a bloodthirsty and ruthless Cartel leader. Rumors circulate amongst the men that she bathes in the blood of her enemies, and I know firsthand what she's done.

Carnage and blood flash before my eyes, but I push the dark memory away.

Not today.

Today, I need to focus on the task at hand. The men scramble to follow her orders, and I take a step forward to follow. Despite the twisted nature of her order, not one man hesitates, as they know what happens if they do.

Her hand clamps on my shoulder, stopping me. "Where do you think you're going?"

"To help."

She shakes her head. "I don't need you to help with that. Come and have breakfast with me."

I clench my jaw. What grows when it's fed but dies when it's watered? I want to ask her that question, but I know best to shut my mouth. Ileana hates riddles. Hatred grows when it's fed but dies when it's watered with love. She has fed my hatred daily for twenty-two years. It consumes me. A dark, intangible entity that fills every void in my soul.

And I'm certain she'll not water it with love, as the red queen doesn't have the capacity. She's soulless. Dead inside. And she's been trying to make me the same. A soldier in her image. While my soul is shattered and fragmented, there are still small pieces she hasn't eradicated.

I bow my head and follow her toward the dining room. Where a table is set, and she takes a seat on one end. I take the chair opposite.

She looks me in the eye but doesn't say a word. Those dark eyes of hers have haunted me since I was a child. Ileana isn't my mother, but she took me as her son and raised me. There's nothing loving about her, though. She's every child's worst nightmare.

She eats her breakfast. Even though my stomach growls in hunger, I don't touch the food. Not until she permits me to do so.

"Eat, Taren."

I grab my fork and tuck into the migas, a traditional Mexican breakfast dish. I know better than to refuse the Red Queen's orders. Following her orders has been ingrained in me since I was a child.

I can feel her eyes on me as I eat, studying my every move. I ignore it and focus on the food. But when she speaks again, her voice cuts through the silence like a knife.

"I've got a job for you," she says, her tone cold and calculating. I know better than to ask what it is. She'll tell me when she's ready, in her own time. "I need you to do what you do best."

Killing and deception. The two skills I excel in are those this woman has honed in me for years. "Which is?" I confirm, wondering which she needs from me.

"There's a charity event next week in Mexico City."

The mention of Mexico City sets me on edge. I haven't stepped foot in the city since I was a child. The harrowing day when I met Ileana Navarro. The day she turned my world upside down. A flash of blood enters my memories, and I force it away.

Not now.

"And you want me to attend?"

She nods in response. "The Estrada Cartel will be there. I want to know why."

Mexico City is a cesspit of crime where no single organization rules. It's open territory and fucking dangerous. I know that all too well. "What do you believe they want?"

Ileana wouldn't send me in there if she doesn't think they're after something valuable. "The city."

My brow furrows. "Mexico City?" I confirm.

I see the irritation heighten as she clenches her jaw. "Of course. What other city would I be talking about?"

"It's impossible. No one has held Mexico City for years."

"It's not impossible, and the North American

leader of the Estrada Cartel is ruthless in his pursuit of more."

Adrik Volkov, who leads the Stateside operations of the Estrada Cartel, is Russian. When I heard the news, I was sure that Pablo Estrada had gone more insane than me. Adrik Volkov forced his hand and took out Pablo's brother before forcing his niece into a marriage she didn't want. The guy is almost as ruthless as Ileana herself, and I think it's shaken her, something I've rarely seen.

"Perhaps," I say, stalling as I consider my next words. "What do you want me do about it?"

"I need you to be my eyes and ears." She stabs her fork into a tomato, the juices spraying everywhere. "As you know, I'm barred from entering the city."

I know that, and for good fucking reason. "Oh, barred, you say? Barred like a cage or barred like a tune we forgot to play?" I tilt my head, grinning at her.

Ileana growls. "I don't want any of your games or riddles this morning, Taren. Keep your mouth shut if you've got nothing constructive to say."

I cut off my words abruptly, swallowing down the rising tide of resentment. Ileana may control my actions, but she could never control my thoughts. I feel the corners of my mouth twitch into a smirk.

"Very well, Ileana." My voice is a low purr, coated with feigned obedience I've mastered over the years. As she turns her attention to her food, my gaze hardens, and my smirk gives way to a grimace.

Her men call me the mad hatter, but there's a method to my madness. You've got to be mad to put up with what I've endured. I can almost taste the bitter bile of hatred for the woman who stole my childhood.

My fingers tap an erratic rhythm on the table, mimicking an orchestra of chaotic thoughts playing in my head. The metallic clink of my rings against the wood echoes in the tense silence.

Ileana clears her throat, breaking the spell. "You'll tell me everything that goes on in the city." Her tone brooks no argument, but I can see the crackle of danger in her eyes. Something has rattled her, and she's looking to regain control.

I nod once, a silent promise to carry out her orders. But as I get up from the table and approach the door, my mind is already churning with my plans. Plans to take back control of my life, no matter the cost.

2

ALICE

The waves crash against the shore as exotic birds chirping fill the air. I take a long sip of my margarita before reclining back on my sun bed and exhaling.

Paradise.

This vacation is exactly what I needed three weeks before the start of my senior year at Brown. It'll be a lot of work to remain top of my class. For now, I can relax and unwind with my best friends.

"This is the life, isn't it?" Luna asks, flicking her ebony hair behind her.

I nod. "Yeah, where's Kali?"

She smirks and nods toward a small cove off the beach where she's wrapped in the arms of a hot Mexican guy.

I shake my head. "Typical Kali."

Blake is paddling on her surfboard but has complained that the waves aren't big enough since we arrived. They're perfect for me. I don't want to be swept under the ocean while trying to take a dip.

Luna chuckles, her green eyes twinkling in the midday sun. "Do you think Kali's new friend knows she can't speak Spanish?"

I laugh, "Probably not, but you know Kali, she'll communicate."

She nods, her gaze drifting back to the ocean. "We're going to miss these days. We'll be stuck in the library soon, buried under piles of books."

"Yeah, I know," I say, sighing, my eyes on the azure blue of the sea. "But for now, let's enjoy the sun, the sea, and the margaritas."

"Cheers to that." She clinks her glass against mine, and we both take a sip.

Blake comes out of the sea, her surfboard under her arm and beautiful golden hair in curls across her shoulders. It's hard to believe she's just been in the sea, as she looks like a fashion model. "Useless again."

Luna rolls her eyes. "Take a breath, will you? We're on vacation. It's about relaxation, not catching the biggest wave."

But Blake's always been a whirlwind of energy, her

feet never quite touching the ground long enough to rest. It's part of her charm, but part of it is her ADHD – always needing to be on the move, always seeking the next rush of adrenaline. She shrugs, drops her board in the sand, and scans the horizon. "Fine. I'll go for a swim."

Luna and I exchange glances as she runs back into the water. "Got to love her," I say.

She nods. "You know, we need to plan our next vacation for winter break." She sighs. "We don't go away enough."

I bite the inside of my cheek because we don't have the money to take many vacations. Luna found this resort cheap online, and at first, I was worried as it's not the safest part of Mexico on the northwest coast. A place where tourists rarely come, but it's even more idyllic because of that.

"Maybe," I say.

She pouts. "Come on, don't be a downer. We'll make it work like we always do."

I can't help but smile at Luna's optimism. She always knows how to find the silver lining in any situation. And she's right. We always make things work, even when money is tight.

But as much as I love traveling and exploring new places, part of me can't help but feel guilty for spending money on vacations when there are so many other things we could use it for. We both work part-time jobs that don't pay well to cover our rent and bills. It took some serious savings to afford this vacation.

"Unless we suddenly get pay rises at Mamachini's, then I'm not sure we have enough time to save by winter break."

She blows out a breath. "Fine, spring break?"

I smile. "It's doable."

"I'm going to hold you to that," she says.

I roll my eyes, noticing that Kali has finally extricated herself from her lover boy's arms and is walking this way.

Luna raises a brow at her as she approaches and flops down on the sunbed next to her. "Having fun?"

Kali shrugs. "He's hot but not the best kisser." She sighs. "Time to move on."

Luna and I both laugh as Kali has impossibly high standards. She's so gorgeous she can have the highest standards she wants, but she's yet to find a man to have more than one date with. There's always something she finds a fault in, whether it be the way he kisses, dresses, or, I kid you, not the way he chews. Kali is as fussy as they come with men.

It'll be a miracle if she ever actually finds a steady boyfriend.

"What's our plans for tonight?" Kali asks, glancing over at me. As always, I take the role of itinerary planner.

"Dinner at the resort."

Kali sighs. "Sounds boring."

"Right?" Luna agrees. "We need to go out and meet some hot young men. We're single and ready to mingle."

I shake my head. "It's safer to remain in the resort. And there are men here at the hotel."

Kali and Luna sigh, exchanging glances.

"She won't budge, will she?" Kali asks.

Luna shakes her head. "Doesn't seem like it."

"You realize I'm right here? And no, I won't budge. We agreed we'd remain in the resort because this area isn't the safest."

"Such a stick in the mud," Kali says, smiling teasingly.

I ignore her comment, shaking my head. "Blake will agree."

"Blake always agrees with you." Luna points out.

It's true. Blake and I have been friends the longest and are more alike out of our friend group. We met in high school in Atlanta and were close friends, but we became even closer when we both attended Brown. And that's when we met Kali and Luna, our two roommates. We've all lived together since our freshman year; it's the start of senior year. The start of the end of an era.

"Because she's sensible," I reply.

"Who's sensible?" Blake asks as she approaches, looking like a goddess that just emerged from the sea.

"You," Kali says, her nose wrinkling. "We wanted to go out drinking tonight, but Alice says we must stay in the resort."

"Agreed," Blake says, smirking at me. "It's far too dangerous to go gallivanting here at night."

Kali and Luna make exaggerated sighing noises, flopping back on their sunbeds.

"I thought we were here to have fun," Kali says.

"We can have fun in the hotel," I suggest. "There's a pool, a bar, a restaurant, and we have each other for company."

Blake grins. "Exactly, isn't that why we're here? To enjoy each other's company before senior year turns us into workaholics."

Luna groans. "Don't remind me. This year is going to be fucking hard."

Despite Luna's carefree attitude and being practically the opposite of a typical nerd in appearance, she majors in computer science. She's a literal genius. It boggles my mind the way she can read and write code. It's like a different language, and she's amazing at it, putting all the nerds to shame as she's one of the top in her class.

Blake is studying psychology, while Kali is studying architecture and has already secured an internship at one of the top architect firms in Boston, Perkins.

On the other hand, I took creative writing because I love it, much to my adoptive parents' disgust. They think I should major in a more academic subject because they can't see what I could get from creative writing. However, I've already secured an internship at Boston's biggest publishing house, Pendulum Press, as a junior editor once I graduate.

I was adopted by them when I was six years old after my mom, my dad, and my sister were killed in a car accident. A truck swerved on the highway after they broke down and hit their car, killing them instantly. The guilt I've felt over it has lived with me since they were on the way to pick me up from school. Jenna, my sister, was only two years old. My memories of all of them are so hazy.

"It's going to be fun. Although I can't believe we don't know where we'll all be in a year," I say, trying to push the thought of my dead family from my mind.

Luna clears her throat. "You and Kali do! At least you two will still be roomies." She sighs heavily. "If I don't find an internship at a software company in Boston, I might have to move away from you guys." She pouts.

"You'll find a job in Boston with no problem," I say, shaking my head.

Unfortunately, it appears software companies are prejudiced as fuck. They see Luna, and they don't believe her credentials. After all, she's five foot seven, with dark hair, beautiful eyes, and gorgeous features because of her mixed heritage. Her mom is Japanese, and her dad is Italian. She looks like a model and gets judged for it, which is ridiculous.

I often feel like I don't fit in with my three friends. They're all so gorgeous. Blake is your typical girl next door with blonde hair, stunning blue eyes, and legs for miles because she's so tall. She's not far off six feet tall. Kali is stunning, too. She has a mixed heritage like Luna. Her mom is Filipino born and bred and her dad is Mexican, but born in Texas.

And then there's me. Boring American girl. Slightly overweight with chestnut brown hair and blue eyes.

"I might have to wear a geek disguise to secure a job. It's like they've never heard of a remotely attractive woman being able to code." She runs a hand through her hair. "They're all fucking assholes. Especially considering I'm better than all of them. And I can hack the shit out of all of their systems."

I must admit she's gone for about ten internships that she's more than qualified for, all of which have turned her down. In high school, she used to hack for money until her parents found out and kicked her out just weeks before she started college. She used the money she saved for her school fees and hasn't spoken to them since. When she enrolled at Brown, she gave up the hacking and now works at the same pizza place as me.

"What about freelance?" Blake suggests sitting on her sun bed and tapping her foot rhythmically on the sand. "There's a high demand for freelance software developers. You might as well make your way if they're being jerks."

Luna contemplates that before nodding. "Maybe. Anything to move to Boston with you guys. Freelance just opens up temptation, though."

The temptation to hack. I know she'd rather have a steady income from a legitimate company.

"What about you, Blake?" I ask, wondering if she's decided what to do.

Her dad has a very high position as a senior surgeon at a hospital in Atlanta, and he's secured her a position as a psychiatrist. However, she's been on the fence about taking it. Her parents have been all about achievements all her life, but they favor her brother, who's taken after his dad and become a heart surgeon. And they often tell her she wouldn't have been able to get where she is without them.

"I'm still trying to work out what to do about the position in Atlanta." She pinches the bridge of her nose. "I know they'll hold it over me if I take it. And then I'd have to be in Atlanta rather than Boston with you guys." She sighs. "It's a great position, though."

Blake looks conflicted, and I sympathize with her dilemma. "I don't know what to do," she says, finally looking up at us. "I don't want to disappoint my parents, but I also want to make my way in life."

Luna reaches over and squeezes her hand. "We'll support you no matter what you decide. Don't let anyone else's expectations dictate your decision."

Blake smiles. "Thanks, I needed to hear that."

"Do you know what?" Kali asks, standing.

"What?" I ask.

"It's time to get more cocktails. This conversation is too serious and this a holiday to forget about anything serious for one week." Kali sets her hands on her hips.

We all chuckle as she looks so stern.

"I'm not joking." She tosses her beach bag over her shoulder. "Come on, we're going to the bar."

She can be so bossy.

But we all grab our bags, following her off the beach toward the bar by the pool.

"What are you having?" Blake asks, probably because Luna and I have been trying out the bar since eleven this morning.

"Margarita, of course. They're damn good."

"Seconded," Luna says.

Blake nods and glances at the bartender. "Three margaritas, and... What do you want, Kali?"

"I'll have a shot of tequila." She glares at me and Luna. "Got to catch up with these alcoholics."

We all laugh.

"And a tequila shot, please," Blake finishes.

The bartender nods his head and goes to get our drinks. We all gaze around the restaurant. It's our first day here, and it seems quiet. There are few men for Kali and Luna to flirt with. Blake and I don't often concern ourselves with hooking up with random guys, and I've not been near a man for a long time. Blake has been helping me get some perspective on my intimacy issues, even though she doesn't know the root cause.

"Where've you gone to?" Blake asks, nudging me.

I shake my head. "Nowhere," I lie, hating that she'll

probably know I'm lying because she's a damn good psychologist.

She's about to speak when a loud noise that sounds worryingly like a gunshot pierces the air.

"What the fuck was that?"

And then there's even more noise that is unmistakable. Machine guns. I stare at the bartender. "What the fuck is going on?"

His eyes are wide as he quickly rushes out from behind the bar. "Run for your lives."

"Shit!" Blake says. "This way." She takes off down toward the beach, and we all follow her, running away from the source of the shooting.

"So much for the resort being safe!" Luna says as we sprint side by side.

I swallow the bile rising in my throat, wondering if we're going to die here in Mexico. It would be a ridiculous price to pay for a cheap holiday. When we get down to the beach, Kali screams. And that's when I see ten men approaching the resort from the beach, all wielding machine guns.

We move to run, but they call out. "Freeze! Or we'll shoot."

We raise our hands above our heads, turning back to face the gunmen. Four of them approach us with their guns lowered while the other men keep them trained on us. They clap handcuffs onto our arms, speaking to each other in Spanish.

I catch some words. Two of the most concerning are *'putas perfectas,'* which means perfect whores. My stomach twists with sickness.

I can't believe that paradise just turned into a nightmare at the flick of a switch. Never ignore your gut, as I had a bad feeling about this holiday before we booked it, and now I wish I'd listened to that feeling. We won't make it home alive.

3
TAREN

*T*he men march back into the house with solemn expressions. Most of these guys don't serve Ileana by choice, much like me.

"How did it go, Carlos?" I ask one of her generals.

His jaw clenches as he meets my gaze. "It's done. Juan has taken four Americans to the basement."

I freeze. "Ileana said no survivors."

"They had nothing to do with the Guerra gang but were staying at their resort. Ileana mentioned she didn't want any tourists involved."

"Why did you kidnap them, then?" I clench my fists by my sides.

"Jorge's orders. He believes they'll fetch us a good price."

Jorge is one of the few men who follows Ileana by

choice. He's as cold and calculated as she is, so he heads her army.

"Very well. I'll go and visit them."

Carlos nods as I turn and head toward the basement, unease settling in the pit of my stomach. Jorge would only spare these women if they were beautiful enough to be put up for auction.

I glare at the door to the basement, wishing I could burn this place to the ground.

Give it time.

How long? How long must I endure this bullshit?

The voice in my head doesn't respond.

As I open the door and descend into the darkness, spiders crawl across my skin as the walls close in on me. Darkness swells within me as I descend the steps into the torture chambers of Ileana Navarro. It's a living, breathing entity that wants to bathe in the blood of our prisoners. The men should have fucking killed the tourists, no matter how much they might fetch.

They'll be all over the news once they're reported missing by their families.

I move around the corner and into the first chamber, where two girls are being held. One with golden curls and green eyes, and the other has olive skin and dark brown eyes. They're both beautiful in their own right. They look at me and cower, their eyes wide with fear, clutching onto each other.

And instantly, I understand why the men *didn't* kill them. They'll fetch a handsome price on the open market, but no doubt they wouldn't mind having them beforehand in their beds. I move to the next chamber, and my steps falter.

The room is dim, the single bulb hanging from the ceiling barely effective, but there she is. Shackled and bound but radiant as a blossom in the moonlight. Her terrified eyes, the color of the clearest skies, meet mine, striking me like a lightning bolt.

I feel like I'm standing at the edge of a precipice, staring into the unknown. The girl's beauty is a paradox, a hideous delight. It cuts through the stench of fear and blood, insinuating itself into the marrow of my madness. I can't help but stand there, entranced, watching her tremble.

I take a step, then another, each footfall echoing ominously. The chains around my little bird's wrists rattle as she instinctively recoils. Her sky-blue eyes grow impossibly wide. Leaning toward her, a smile plays on my lips, and my voice echoes in the corridor as I speak, "What's seen in the middle of March and April that can't be seen at the beginning or end of either?" Confusion flashes in her eyes, her brows furrowing as she tries to interpret the riddle.

"W-What?"

The sound of her fragile voice is a beautiful melody amid chaos. I ignore her confusion, the question hanging in the air between us. My voice barely more than a whisper, "And who might you be little bird?" I lean closer, the cold steel of the bars pressing against my face.

Her lip trembles as she tightens her grasp on her friend. "Alice," she whispers.

Alice.

I don't ask for her friend's name. She doesn't interest me in the slightest.

A dangerous spark ignites in my heart at the thought of having her to myself, even though I know Ileana wouldn't allow it.

I watch her shrink into the shadows. "Here's another riddle for you, Alice," I purr. "What dances without legs, whispers without voice, bites without teeth, and dies without life?"

She shakes her head. "I-I don't know."

My eyes narrow as I lean in closer, my face inches away from hers, and if it weren't for the bars, I'd have her in my hands. "Think, little bird."

She closes her eyes, breathing in short gasps as she

tries to solve my riddle. But I know she won't be able to, not in her state of terror. I lean back, watching her struggle.

Fear can cripple even the brightest minds, but whether she is bright remains to be seen. She intrigues me. With her wide, innocent eyes and trembling lips, she exudes a certain vulnerability that I can't resist.

"Come closer," I demand.

She hesitates, her eyes wide. And then, finally she relents and steps closer to the bars.

I reach through them and touch her cheek gently with the back of my hand, relishing in the softness of her skin. "It's wind," I say softly, my voice devoid of the menacing tone I'd used earlier. "The wind dances without legs, whispers without voice, and bites without teeth. And it dies when it stops blowing."

I watch as a flicker of understanding passes through her eyes before being drowned out by fear again. She pulls away from my touch, huddling closer to her friend for protection. I glance at the friend. She, too, is beautiful with dark ebony hair and tanned skin. However, no one's beauty outshines Alice's.

Her eyes are a brilliant shade of sky blue, with a spark of determination flickering in their depths. Each strand of her wavy brown hair shimmers in the scarce light in the room, giving her an ethereal glow. Her lips are full, tempting me to erase the fear etched onto her face and replace it with red-hot desire.

Her skin is as delicate as porcelain, so perfect it could easily crack. She stands out like a diamond amidst stones. In all her fragile beauty, Alice has claimed a corner of my mind in two seconds flat. A part of my mind I'd believed was impervious to distractions.

"W- What are you going to do with us?"

I tilt my head, considering her question. A whirl-wind of chaotic thoughts and images grace my mind, many too perverse to put into words. I would delight in breaking this girl and putting her back together again, making her fit against my broken pieces like a jigsaw puzzle.

"Your eyes are open, and I'm there. Close them. I'm there, too. What am I?"

The other girl snorts. "That's easy. It's the dark."

I glare at her. "Did I ask you?"

She retreats a little at the tone of my voice. "No."

"Then stay out of it." I turn my attention back to Alice. "Shame you didn't answer any of my riddles, little bird. Maybe next time."

I lean closer, wishing the bars weren't between us and counting the heartbeats that drum against my chest. "Come here," I demand again.

She steps forward and I reach through and cup her chin, forcing her eyes to mine. My thumb brushes across her trembling lips, and she visibly swallows. "You're an enigma, little bird. And I intend to unravel every layer until you're completely in my grasp."

She looks at me with wide eyes, fear, and curiosity, battling for dominance. "What do you want?"

I lean in even closer, my face squashed against the bars. "You."

Her breath hitches again, but her gaze has a spark of defiance. Despite her fear, she refuses to cower. I'm intrigued by her strength and resolve. "What do you intend to do with me?"

I smile, whispering in the space between us, "Whatever I please."

I can feel the tremors running through her body, but I also sense something else. Desire. She may be afraid of me, but a part of her also wants me as much. And I will use that to my advantage.

I release her chin, breaking our intimate connection. "But for now, I've business to attend to."

As I turn to leave, I can't help but wonder how long it'll take for her to succumb to me. How long before she realizes she belongs to me, body and soul? The only spanner in the works will be Ileana. She's selfish and wants me all to herself. If she knew I had eyes for Alice, she'd murder her in front of me.

A foreign, possessive feeling stirs at the thought of Alice in danger. A primal instinct drives a need to protect what's mine. I've never felt a pull like this, a powerful urge to claim, possess, and protect.

It's as if Alice has suddenly become a vital part of my existence, and the mere thought of her being harmed raises a fierceness within me that could burn entire worlds. I'll have to tread carefully, keeping Ileana and Alice in the dark until I can ensure Alice's safety and claim her openly.

4

ALICE

"*W*hat the fuck was that?" Luna asks, eyes as wide as saucers.

I shake my head, my eyes pinned to where that man questioned us, or more like me. He barely looked at Luna. It was clear from one look in his eyes he wasn't sound of mind, but when he spoke. I tremble. The memory of his voice haunts me.

"I can't believe this is happening." Luna's voice breaks as she speaks.

I reach for her hand, squeezing. "We need to get out of here," I say, my voice barely above a whisper.

"Right, but how?" She signals to the bars of our cage.

Little bird.

The man's voice echoes in my head. I'm a bird trapped in a cage.

"Luna? Alice?" Blake's voice catches our attention, and then we notice a large crack in the wall between our cells.

I rush over to it. "Oh my God. Are you guys okay?"

"Shaken." She glances at Kali, who's rocking back and forth, clutching her legs into her chest on the floor. "Kali is more shaken than me."

I nod. "We need to get out of here before that man returns."

"But how?" Luna asks, her voice laced with desperation.

I glance around the cell, searching for any escape routes. And then I spot a small vent in the ceiling. "Up there," I say, pointing to the vent.

Luna purses her lips. "How small do you think we are?"

I admit it looks like a tiny gap, and it would be a squeeze, but we're out of options. "We need to at least try. Give me a boost."

The look on her face is one of pure horror. "Or don't, and we can just rot in here and die."

She sighs, crouching down for me to put my foot in her hands. "This day is just getting worse and worse."

"I think giving me a boost will be the highlight of your day if we don't get out of here." My voice is strained as I climb onto her shoulders and reach the vent.

"Fuck, you're heavier than you look."

I grit my teeth as I've never been stick-thin like her, so I don't appreciate the comment. I pry the grill from the vent and pass it to Luna. And then I stick my head into the hole, looking on either side. It's dark and thinner on the inside than I imagined.

Luna's hands are shaking beneath my feet. "What do you think?"

I shake my head. "It's tight. And I don't know where it leads, but what choice do we have?"

"Okay, try to fit inside."

My heart hammers against my rib cage as I brace my hands on the metal and use my severely lacking upper body strength to pull myself up. I struggle, trying to get my legs in behind me. This looks so much easier in the movies.

"Are you sure you can get up there?" Luna asks.

I grind my teeth, probably looking like a fish out of water, as I cannot pull myself into the vent. The metal grates scrape against my skin, but I push through the discomfort. Suddenly, a loud bang echoes throughout the vent, causing me to lose my grip. I land on the concrete floor with a thud.

"Shit," I cry.

Luna rushes over to my side. "Oh God, are you okay?"

"Someone's coming!" Blake warns.

The vent cover remains on the floor, and I quickly grab it, pushing it behind me. The man who was here merely twenty minutes ago reappears.

"Alice, Alice, Alice." He shakes his head. "Did you think we don't have cameras here, little bird?"

Cameras.

I glance around and spot one in the corner, feeling like a fool for not checking that first.

"And now you're injured, aren't you? Did you break your wing as you fell?"

I glare at him and force myself to my feet despite the pain. "No." I'm badly bruised, for sure.

"I think I'm going to check." He's holding the keys to the prison cell and slides them into the lock.

Luna steps forward.

The man stills, dark eyes narrowing. "Stay back." He glares at her. "You don't want to discover what happens if you try to escape." He flashes a row of perfectly white teeth, which look stark against his gorgeous, tanned skin.

Luna and I both shudder as he continues to unlock the door. The click of the lock makes my heart pound harder. An instinct to fight and escape claws at every muscle in my body. I feel like I'm one of those idiots you shout at on the TV not to attempt an escape because there's practically no chance of it working out, but it's a lot different when you're in the situation.

As he slides open the door, I bide my time. Once he steps inside, I'll make my move. Luna meets my gaze, shaking her head. She can read what I intend to do, which gives me pause.

"Whatever you're thinking, little bird, don't do it." His voice snaps my attention back to him. "Come here," he demands.

I accept that there's no escape. This man would overpower me in a heartbeat if I tried to get away. Releasing a shaky breath, I force one foot before the other and walk to him.

Once within a foot, he grabs my hair and yanks my head back.

"Fly out of here, but there's nowhere for you to go," he breathes, gazing down at me with that same manic look I'd seen earlier. "In the cage, a bird might sing, not of joy, but of longing. It yearns for the sky that it sees but cannot touch. Each bar in its cage, a cruel reminder of its clipped wings." He moves his hands to my shoulder blades and moves them in circles. "Where are your wings?"

I glare at him, wondering if he's insane.

He releases my hair and grabs my wrist, yanking me out of the cell and shutting it closed behind us. I glance back at Luna to see she's staring after me in wide-eyed shock.

A tear spills from my eyes down my cheek. He stops when we're out of her sight and pushes me against a wall.

"Are you hurt?"

I shrug. "No, I'll be a bit bruised, but live."

His eyes flash. "Turn around."

When I don't move, he forces me around and hikes my beach dress up, making me tense. "You'll be badly bruised. My Alice." And then I feel his lips at the center of my spine, making my heart kick into gear for an utterly different reason. "Let me kiss it better, little bird."

I shudder as his lips move from the base of my spine right until he's kissing the back of my neck.

"Does it feel better now?" he murmurs.

I can hardly think with this madman behind me, making me feel how no one should feel in my position. My thighs are slick with arousal as he continues to press his lips against my neck. "Please," I breathe.

I don't know if I'm begging him to stop or for more.

He stills. "Please, what?"

"I-I don't know."

He chuckles, the sound a little crazy but also deep and erotic. "It's perplexing, isn't it? An enigma encased within the human psyche."

"What is?" I ask, drawn into this man like a moth to a flame.

"Desire," he breathes. "It treads the line between dread and longing."

He's right. I should feel dread right now, but that sensation only heightens my longing. "What are you doing to me?"

His breath skates over my skin as he laughs softly. "Nothing, little bird. Your own carnal craving paints your confusion. I'm only stoking the fires that already simmer beneath your skin."

He forces me around, gazing at me with an intensity that could bring empires to their knees. I think he might kiss me, but he doesn't. We're suspended there, gazing into each other's eyes. The unbelievable thing is that I want him to kiss me. I want to delve into this man's madness. At least it's better than facing my bleak reality.

"Taren!" A man shouts, drawing the man's attention from me. "You aren't supposed to let the prisoners out of the cell."

Taren.

That must be this man's name.

He puts distance between us, tearing his eyes from me. "Are you questioning my methods, Pedro?"

The other guard cowers at the lethal tone of Taren's voice, shaking his head. "No, it's just—"

Taren grabs Pedro by the throat and squeezes hard, lifting him a couple of inches off the floor. "You're no one," he growls, nostrils flaring and eyes full of barely contained madness. "I don't expect to be questioned. What would the red queen say if she knew?"

The red queen.

I wonder if that's another of his riddles.

Pedro's eyes flicker shut as his face turns pale. Finally, he releases Pedro. He drops to the floor in a heap, inhaling a forceful breath of oxygen. His eyes are wide as he clutches his throat.

"I was finished with her, anyway." A paradoxical calm to his tone, considering he almost strangled a guy to death. "Come, little bird, back in your cage." He grabs my wrist and yanks me toward the cell where Luna is waiting, looking more terrified than ever.

When she sees I'm okay, some of the fear dissipates.

Taren shoves me in roughly and locks the door, barely glancing at me again. I watch as he retreats, his shirt clinging to his taut, muscular back.

Luna rushes to me. "Thank God, I thought…" She trails off, as we both know what she thought. She thought I was dead, and for a second, I did, too. Until Taren touched me as if I were the most precious thing in the world to him.

It makes no sense, but that's how he makes me feel.

"I know, so did I." I swallow.

"Are you okay, Alice?" Blake asks.

I walk back over to the crack and nod. "Yeah. How's Kali holding up?"

Kali walks to join Blake. "I'm shitting myself."

"I think we all are," Luna says.

I nod in response, but a part of me isn't terrified. A part of me is intrigued by the man who holds us captive. Taren is an enigma I want to learn more about. Even though my common sense screams at me to run whenever he's close.

5

TAREN

*I*leana enters the kitchen, where I'm skinning a rabbit I caught earlier.

Her brow scrunches, and she shakes her head. "We have servants for that."

I clench my jaw. "You know I enjoy it."

"I hear you took a prisoner from her cell today."

Fucking Pedro.

I can't do anything around here without people ratting on me. He was the guard on duty when I let her out. "What of it?" I don't take my eyes off the rabbit, peeling away the skin from the flesh. What I'd give to peel the skin from her flesh while she screams in agony. It would be pure perfection.

"Why did you remove her from her cell?"

I shrug. "The prisoner fell. I was checking for

injuries." I know my actions aren't synonymous with my normal ways. If I caught a prisoner attempting to escape, normally, I'd break their kneecaps to ensure they can't try again.

"She was trying to escape, Taren."

I drop my knife with a clatter, blood splattering my shirt. "If you've got something to say, then say it." I lift my eyes to meet hers.

Her jaw clenches. "It's just very unlike you."

"About the event in Mexico City next week."

"What of it?" she asks, looking slightly surprised by the sudden change of subject.

"I'll take that prisoner with me as my date."

Her brow furrows deeper. "No chance."

"She's attractive and quiet, the perfect accomplice to help me blend in."

Ileana's jaw clenches. "Take the other."

I must tread carefully here, as Ileana can't know how I feel about Alice. "The others are too loud and foul-mouthed. The one who fell from the vent will be more suitable." I tilt my head. "After all, we need to train them if they're going to sell for a lot of money at auction."

Ileana raises a brow. "You don't normally concern yourself with the training."

"Perhaps I'm bored and want a new challenge."

She laughs. "I must admit, it's been a long time since you had female contact. Fine. Take her with you, but make sure you keep her close."

I clench my jaw. "Of course, I'm not an idiot." Ileana thinks I want to fuck her. While that's partly true, it's not the extent of my desire. Alice belongs by my side. She belongs to me.

Alice isn't just another prisoner or another asset to be sold to the highest bidder. She has a fire that matches the chaos within me. I want to harness that fire, not put it out. I crave to feel its heat, to lose myself in its intensity.

"No, you're not." Ileana's lips curve into a smile. "I'm sure you have everything under control."

I nod, knowing that she trusts me implicitly. A grave fucking mistake because trust is a double-edged sword. The fragile nature of trust makes it a treacherous path to tread. Ileana must underestimate me if she believes she's snuffed all humanity from my soul.

A flashback of blood and chaos enters my mind, but I force it away.

Not now.

"I've made preparations. The jet will be ready to take you to the city on Wednesday morning. You'll return the following evening."

I bow my head. "Fine."

She turns to leave. "And Taren?"

"Yes?"

"Don't fuck it up. I know Mexico City has... memories for you, but that is the past." She watches me with cold eyes. "We must look to the future."

The audacity. I'm shocked Ileana would bring it up, considering she's the reason for those dark, inescapable memories.

I take a deep breath, forcing myself to nod. "Agreed."

She leaves, and I'm alone with my thoughts. I tear the final piece of skin from the flesh and toss it aside, gazing at the blood covering the granite worktop. The flashbacks try to creep into my mind, but I shut them down. I've kept them in check for twenty-two years, but they've become more persistent. As if my mind is demanding that I take my revenge and end this insanity.

It's not the right time yet.

To my surprise, my mind returns to sky-blue eyes and porcelain skin. Alice.

She will be the key to my salvation. A fragment of sanity in my realm of madness. In her, I might find the strength to face the ghosts of my past and remove the collar around my neck.

I string the rabbit above the worktop, knowing

Daniela will appreciate my work when she makes dinner this evening. She's always appreciative when I hunt fresh meat, which tastes better than anything she buys from the grocery store. And while Ileana insists that it's below me to skin the animal, I disagree. She keeps me on a leash more often, making it impossible to find an outlet for my rage.

Five days from now, I'll be on a jet with my new obsession. Alice. I sigh heavily as images of her bound and gagged on my bed with her eyes wide in fear grace my mind. A throb ignites between my thighs at the heady image. I will feed off her fear and bask in it. Watch as that fear turns to pure fire, and she comes apart for me repeatedly.

I lean over the counter, bracing myself against the storm of desire threatening to pull me under. Desire is something I rarely feel. I've been under Ileana's thumb for too long, and it's turned me into a shell of a man. And yet, the moment I saw Alice, I felt that part of me coming rushing back in full force.

Wednesday can't come soon enough. I can't see her until then, as I don't trust myself or anyone else here. Ileana must never know the extent of my desires for the pretty little prisoner in our basement. Otherwise, chaos will ensue.

* * *

Sleep eludes me as I stare mindlessly at the stained ceiling.

It's been two days since I met Alice, and keeping away from her is proving difficult.

Alice may be a lamb among wolves, but she's ensnared me in her trap.

I grab my cell phone off the nightstand and check the security cameras, sighing when I see her beautiful form curled up on the hay. The desire to visit her is clawing at me so deeply. Watching isn't enough. I need to touch her again. Feel her soft skin against mine and check how badly she's bruised after her fall.

Damn it.

I climb out of bed, knowing that if word of my visiting a prisoner gets to Ileana, it would be catastrophic for all involved. The guard on duty today is Andre, and he's not as much of a stickler for the rules as Pedro. I'll pass him a bribe, and he'll keep my secret. He probably wouldn't look too much into it, as most don't understand the method to my madness.

I throw on a pair of sweatpants and a shirt, grabbing my copy of the cell keys and some gel to apply to her bruises. And then I leave my room, descending into hell itself. It's unusual for me to visit the basement by choice. I spent far too much time down here as a child by force.

And yet, the descent doesn't feel as heavy as usual. Because my sweet Alice is waiting for me. Andre's brow furrows as he looks up from his cell phone. "What are you doing down here, Taren?"

"I need to speak with the prisoners."

He raises a brow. "At—" He looks at his watch. "Three in the morning?"

I nod. "Here's a hundred dollars. No one hears of this, got it?"

His eyes light up when he sees the cash. "Of course." He salutes me. "Your secret is safe with me. Have fun." He winks.

I ignore him and walk toward Alice's cell. She's still fast asleep, and so is her friend. I grab the cell bars and squeeze, my knuckles turning white. Fate. In its cruelty, it has bound me to Alice, a radiant beam of innocence and light, only to have her ensnared in the clutches of my nemesis.

I dig the cell door key from the pocket in my sweatpants. "Alice," I breathe her name, hoping she'll hear me.

She doesn't stir.

I clench my jaw and open the door, tiptoeing toward her. I don't intend to wake her friend. Her friend is beautiful, and I can admire her beauty, but for me, it pales compared to Alice. Matias and Thiago, on the other hand, will eat the poor girl alive. In fact, they'll want all the girls, including Alice. I need to protect her from them.

Approaching silently, I crouch down and place a hand over Alice's mouth. Her eyes shoot open, panic alight in those sky-blue eyes.

Gently, I use my other hand to put a finger over my mouth. After a few beats, some panic eases, and she nods. Alice trusts me. It might be a fatal mistake to trust a madman like me.

"Come with me," I breathe, my voice barely a whisper.

She nods as I release my hand from her mouth and straighten. Alice stands and follows me out of the cell, which I lock to ensure her friend doesn't wake up and try to escape.

"What are you doing here?" she whispers.

I push her further into the basement where I'd kissed her bruise the other day. "To check your bruising." I force her around and pull her dress up, groaning at the purple and black across her back. "This looks painful, little bird." I drag my fingers over the bruise, and she shivers.

"It's okay."

I shake my head, hating seeing her hurt. "No, seeing you in pain is like watching the sun being swallowed by the darkness. It's unbearable." I trace the edge of the bruise with a gentleness I didn't know I possessed. "You're my daylight, Alice. And I can't bear to see my daylight eclipsed."

"Taren," she breathes my name, and I tense.

"Say that again," I demand.

"Taren," she says my name again, only it's more hesitant this time.

"I like how it sounds when you say my name."

She tries to turn around to face me, but I firmly push her against the wall.

"No. Stay still." I pull the gel out of my pocket and put some on my hand. "I've got something for the bruising."

Gently, I rub the product into the bruised area. The only bruises I want to see on my little bird are those I've inflicted, which were born from passion. And yet, I know if we're going to make this out with our lives, I'll see her harmed more before our salvation.

A soft moan escapes her lips as my fingers dance down her spine. "Taren, why?"

Why? Why am I treating this pretty bird so well?

Because she's mine.

"Why?" I repeat. "It's the ultimate question, isn't it?"

Once I'm finished, I yank her around to face me. "Pretty little Alice."

Her sky-blue eyes dilate with desire as she places her hand on my chest, making me tense. "Can you help me?"

I tilt my head. "Does Alice desire me, or does she just desire her freedom?" I grab a fistful of her hair and yank her head back. "Do you want to use me?" My nostrils flare with anger at the thought. "Do you think I can free you, and you'll be safe?"

Her throat bobs, but that flicker of desire burns brightly. "No," she breathes.

"Then what do you think I can give you, little bird?"

She bites her bottom lip, drawing my eyes to their fullness. Her breath hitches. "Hope," she murmurs, her voice barely above a whisper. "Hope that I can feel something again."

Feel something again.

Why doesn't my little bird feel?

All these questions swirl around in my mind. "Tell me why you don't feel," I demand.

Her jaw clenches and a wall of steel covers the emotion that was blazing with her eyes a moment again. "I can't."

"No?" My voice is an icy whisper, a mirror of the

steel in her eyes. "Or won't?" I watch as she remains ice-cold under my gaze. I release her hair and cradle her face instead. "I'll crack you open and learn your secrets. No matter how hard you try to hide them."

Her eyes flicker with fear and defiance, her lips parting. "Crack me open then," she dares.

I smirk, intrigued all the more by my little bird. Alice is as enigmatic as the moon, revealing only glimpses of her secrets yet enticing me deeper into her mystery. "Do you like danger?"

Her chest heaves with heavy breaths as she nods. "Yes."

"Good, because you're provoking a very dangerous man." I grab her hips and push her back against the wall, careful not to be too forceful because of her bruise. She winces at the contact. "How shall I open you up?" I press my lips to her neck and bite hard enough to hurt, making her yelp at the contact. "Shall I bite you open?"

Alice doesn't push me away. She threads her fingers in my hair and yanks me closer. "Yes."

Intriguing. Dark and delicious.

How has this creature become so dark?

I bite her shoulder hard and then suck, wanting to leave my mark on her despite the danger. "Alice," I breathe her name, my cock throbbing against her stomach. "Too tempting." I kiss her collarbone and then nip it hard, making her moan. "I want to have you until the stars burn out and the world fades to nothing until all that remains is the echo of our bodies colliding in the universe's silence."

"Please," she breathes.

She doesn't realize my meaning. She's full of desire right now. Desperate to feel, but I don't know why. I want her forever. I want her for eternity. I want to drown in her, and until she loves me the way I love her, I won't give her what she wants.

"Not right now, little bird."

She growls in frustration, and I smile.

"Are you a little bird or an angry cat?" I pull back and gaze at her, noticing the irritation in her sky-blue eyes.

"Why are you doing this to me?" she asks.

I take a step back, and her gaze dips to the thick outline of my cock, pressing through the tight gray sweatpants I'm wearing. "What am I doing, Alice?"

"Teasing me," she breathes, her eyes still fixed on the outline of my cock. "Please, Taren."

I arch a brow. "Why do you want it?"

She shakes her head. "I can't explain it."

"Then I can't fuck you, little bird." I tilt my head. "Not like this. Not here."

Alice's brow furrows. "Then when?"

"When you open your heart to me."

She looks even more confused.

"I need you to understand that this isn't purely physical," I add.

Her chest rises and falls with deep breaths. "That makes no sense. You don't know me."

I smirk. "I beg to differ. I might not know your favorite color or the type of music that makes your heart flutter, but I've seen your soul bare, felt the depths of your passion, and the rawness of your vulnerability. I know the rhythm of your heartbeat and the taste of your unspoken words." I move closer, stroking her cheek. "Now it's time for us to part."

I grab her wrist, pull her back to the cell, and open the door. And before I push her inside, I pull her against me one last time to memorize her feel and scent. A mixture of sweet vanilla essence and a natural, earthy fragrance that's uniquely hers. "Don't forget me," I breathe, kissing her cheek. "Goodbye for now." I shut the door and lock her away.

And then I walk away, feeling trapped in a cage of my making. It's a labyrinth, an inescapable maze of contrarieties in which I find myself, a prisoner no less bound than Alice in her cold, steel cage.

6

TAREN

*T*he siren of the alarm clock assaults my ears. It wasn't necessary to set it this morning as I haven't slept at all. Thoughts of Alice have consumed my mind since the day I set eyes on her, and with our trip to Mexico City looming, sleep was an impossibility. The storm within me is impossible to tame.

As I turn over in the bed, my cock throbs incessantly. It's been like this since we met, but I ignore it. Instead, I grab my cell phone from the nightstand and open the security camera app.

And there she is. My little bird. She sleeps on a hay bale in the corner of the cell, looking perfectly peaceful considering her situation. I often watch her when I'm alone, basking in her strength.

Her beauty is an enigma, a riddle wrapped in the mystery of a moonlit night. It's like a cryptic sonnet penned by a long-forgotten bard, every line a testament to her grace, yet each stanza a testament to the paradox of her existence. Like a beautifully crafted cipher, her beauty is as alluring as puzzling. It enthrals and ensnares me yet leaves me yearning for the key to decode it.

"I will crack you, my little bird," I murmur before shutting off the screen and tossing the phone onto the nightstand.

It's been three days since my last visit to her cell, three days since she begged me to make her feel again. Trying to stay away has been hell, but today is the day. We'll spend over twenty-four hours in each other's presence. We won't be entirely alone. Ileana wouldn't let me go into the lion's den without backup. Alex will be on the trip, but I'm not worried about him. He can't wait to hit the strip clubs of Mexico City and told me so himself.

The one-week holding period for the girls is almost up. Which means they'll soon learn the full extent of the horror they've fallen into. Ileana has a rule that all prisoners must be left in solitude with little food and water for a week before we either start their training program or torture, depending on who the prisoner is.

A technique specifically designed to break a prisoner's spirit before we even start to work on them. It's amazing what solitude can do to a person, but the difference with these girls is they've had each other. Something Ileana doesn't normally allow, but we're low on holding space.

The jet will take off at eleven o'clock from a private runway in Ensenada, at least one hour's drive from here, so I need to get ready. And then I need to collect my little bird.

I'm unsure what Alice and her friends were thinking about vacationing to a dangerous part of Mexico. There are a lot of cheap resorts, but if that's the reason, they risked their lives for a cheap holiday, which is true madness. And they say I'm as mad as a hatter.

I climb out of bed and head for the adjoining bathroom, turning on the shower and leaning over the sink counter while waiting for the water to warm. Alice is a distraction I don't need. Everything I've been planning for years is so close I can taste it, yet she clouds my judgment.

I pull my briefs off and step under the spray of the

water, running my hands down my stomach to my solid cock. I'm aching for release. It's been like this since I met Alice, but I refuse to masturbate like a teenager. Instead, I ignore it and focus on washing the rest of my body.

Once I'm washed, I shut off the faucet and step out, grabbing my thick white towel and wrapping it around my waist. My walk-in closet is stocked with hundreds of designer suits. I pick a black pair of pants and a white shirt, but opt for a burgundy dress jacket and my solid gold rabbit cuff-links.

Ileana would disapprove of my mismatched attire, but she knows I don't conform to social norms. I can count on one hand the number of times I've worn a matching suit jacket and pants.

I glance at the ties. The idea of wearing one is suffocating. Even so, I pick a black bow tie and throw it into my luggage and a purple handkerchief to fold into my jacket pocket. Once I'm sure I've finished packing, I shut the suitcase and place it outside the door for the chauffeur to collect.

And then I turn my mind to my obsession. What is an obsession? An unhealthy fixation or a passionate pursuit that fuels our existence? I don't know, but I'm sure my obsession with my little bird is a danger to everything I've worked for.

I walk down the stairs and descend into the basement, finding the darkness easier again today. Perhaps because I know of the light that awaits me below.

My Alice.

My little bird.

My queen.

It's eerily quiet in the basement. Quieter than normal. The two girls who arrived with Alice are in the cell next door, fast asleep, clutching each other tightly. Only true bonds can survive the kind of peril and darkness these girls are to be subjected to. It'll test them and break them.

As I move past that cell and to Alice's, my heart pounds harder.

She's also asleep on the makeshift bed of hay in the corner. Her friend is sleeping next to her. I watch her for a while, her chest rising and falling evenly. She's so beautiful and peaceful as she sleeps easy, unaware of what might await her in the coming days. I wonder what her dreams are made of.

As I watch her, I can't help but think back to the day I kissed her skin. So small and fragile, like a delicate bird that could break easily beneath me. But a fire in her eyes captured my attention when she turned round. A fire that told me she feels this as keenly as I do.

"Alice," I say softly, hoping not to wake her friends.

Her eyes shoot open, meeting mine. "Taren?"

My name from her lips is exquisite. "Yes, little bird. It's me. Come here."

She carefully climbs off the bed, ensuring she doesn't wake her friend. Her hips sway temptingly as she walks toward the bars, willingly walking toward the devil. Alice places her hands around the bars, staring at me. "What is it?"

"You're coming with me."

Her expression turns cautious, and she takes a step back. "Where?"

"The where isn't important."

"I can't leave my friends," she says, gazing back at her dark-haired friend sleeping deeply.

"You'll return to them soon enough. I just have a task for you."

She pulls her bottom lip between her teeth and then nods. "Okay."

I smile because I don't need her permission but want her to come by choice. I unlock her cell and usher her out.

As we walk together through the dark corridors, I can't help but feel a sense of excitement. Alice will be beside me when I face my demons in Mexico City. With her close, I feel I can accomplish anything.

First, I need to get my little bird ready to face the

corruption of Mexican politics. Alice has to blend in seamlessly, but the good thing about birds is they're good at hiding in plain sight.

Alice is about to tread into this serpent's nest with me, unaware of the venom that courses through its veins. The shadows of Mexico City are long and deep, waiting to swallow us whole.

7

ALICE

*T*aren drags me into a bedroom, making my stomach roll.

What is he going to do with me?

His dark eyes meet mine. "Strip."

I shudder and cross my arms over my chest. "Why?"

A muscle in his jaw contracts. "Strip now."

I may still have the fight in me, but the command in his voice is like a knife pressing against my ribcage. My power to ignore is nonexistent as I take off my dress and underwear, standing before him, exposed and vulnerable. I look into his eyes, and the flames in them burn me. Swallowing hard, I cross my arms over my chest to at least hide my breasts.

"No," he growls, marching forward and yanking my arms down. "I want to see you."

A tremor of fear travels from my head to my toes. I'm frozen like a statue. Too scared to even breathe as he gazes at me like a hungry predator.

Are the events of two years ago about to repeat themselves?

I feel flashbacks trying to resurface, but I push them away.

Not now. I can't go there. I need to be strong.

"Are you scared, little bird?" he murmurs, his fingers dancing over the skin at my collarbone. "Do you want to fly away?" His fingers move lower, brushing against my nipple. "Oh, that's right. You can't because your wings are broken."

I shiver, hating that I'm standing before a madman right now. The way he talks isn't normal, and his eyes have an unreadable expression as he stares at me, his fingers moving over my skin.

"Such pretty feathers you have." He squeezes my right nipple hard, and I gasp, jumping back in shock. He chuckles. "I'm going to have fun playing with you."

Fuck.

This man could rape me, and there's nothing I can do. I'm locked in a room with a maniac. I admit I had a lapse of judgment the other day when he tended to my bruises. At that moment, I wanted him to fuck me. I was practically begging, but I've come to my senses now. I've got no idea what this man is truly capable of.

"What do you want?" I ask, hoping somehow I can reason with him.

He tilts his head, gazing into my eyes which such intensity it makes me wish I hadn't spoken. "A beautiful little bird," he muses. Those dark eyes flash with desire. "My beautiful little bird."

I shudder. "I'm not yours."

His smirk widens. "Not yet, but all in good time." He steps back, and his eyes move across my body, assessing. And then he rubs a hand across his crotch, drawing my eyes to the straining fabric barely containing his erection. "So hard. Damn it. You, little Alice, make me hard."

My thighs clench at the same time fear churns my stomach. "W-What are you going"—

"No questions." He steps closer, my heart hammering erratically. "Is my little bird wet?"

I shake my head, but it's a lie. A man like this, so dark and twisted, excites me for all the wrong reasons. My body has been broken for a couple of years now, ever since the *incident.* A shiver skates up my spine as memories of the cold floor against my face flood my mind, but I push it away.

"Are you lying to me?" he asks, his fingers dancing over my bare nipples, making them tighten painfully. "Shall I find out?"

"No, Taren, please."

There's a flash in his eyes when I use his name. "I wanted to hear you say my name," he breathes. "Such a pretty voice. I bet you scream so well."

My throat bobs as my eyes dart around the room, searching for exits. There are none. Even the windows on the right side of the room have large metal bars across them.

"There's no escape." He grabs my wrist suddenly and yanks me toward a door on the left, dragging me into an opulent bathroom with a huge tub and a shower big enough for an orgy.

He turns on the faucet in the shower and strips off his own clothes until he's naked. Flames fan across my skin at the sight of his cock. It's huge, and so hard it's pressed flat against his muscular abs. He has tattoos across both arms, adding to his rugged allure. And I notice the burns and scars across his abdomen too.

I swallow hard, trying to ignore the throb between my thighs.

"Get in," he orders.

"Please, Taren. I don't want to have sex with you."

He tilts his head, amusement flashing into his dark eyes. "Who said anything about sex, little bird?"

My eyes instinctively dart to his thick cock. "It didn't need to be said."

He chuckles. His laugh is deep and manic. "Don't worry. I may be attracted to you very much, but I won't fuck you right now."

Relief fills me as I feel my muscles relax an inch. However, my body craves this man's touch.

"Now, be a good little bird and get in."

I walk into the shower and under the warm, soothing spray. A moan escapes my lips as after God knows how long in that dank, disgusting cell, a shower feels like heaven.

And then I stiffen when I feel his warmth behind me, turning to face him. "I thought you said—"

"I'm going to wash you." He grabs a loofah off the rack on the wall and a bottle of soap, lathering it up. And then, slowly, he rubs it across my shoulders, taking time to massage the soap into my skin. He moves it over my breasts next. His touch is firm yet gentle, making goosebumps erupt all over my body. I close my eyes against the sensation, trying to control the tremors of fear and excitement coursing through me.

"What's a bird not in the sky that can swim in the

ocean and stay dry?" Taren speaks, making my heart hammer. And then he uses the loofah between my thighs, making me jolt in shock as it brushes against my clit.

My breathing becomes labored as I open my mouth to answer, but I don't know it. Whenever I'm around this man, my mind turns blank. And especially with him touching me. It feels so apart from our roles of me being the captive and him being the captor.

Why the fuck would he wash me?

"Do you know it?" He chuckles softly. "You should, since you're a bird."

"No," I breathe as he puts down the loofah and grabs a bottle of shampoo off the rack.

"Turn around."

I do as he says, and he lathers the shampoo into my hair. His fingers massage my scalp, and an unexpected moan escapes my lips.

He groans. "The answer is a shadow."

Why does he like to speak in riddles so much?

This man is the most intriguing and terrifying man I've ever met, and I hate I want to know more about him. I shouldn't because he's keeping me captive and holds my life in his hands.

He grabs the additional shower head and washes

the shampoo from my hair. "Turn and face me," he orders once he's done.

I turn around to look at him, and the desire in his eyes threatens to burn me where I stand. "What now?" I murmur so quietly it's barely audible above the water.

"Time to go."

"Go where?" I ask.

His smirk widens. "You'll see."

I watch as he turns and walks out of the shower, surprised that he didn't touch me beyond washing me. A part of me is disappointed, which is utterly fucked up. But then, I've been fucked up for a while now. My mind receding into the darkest depths ever since...

I draw in a deep breath, trying to forget my memories. Taren coaxes them to the surface, which scares me more than anything else. Once I leave the shower, he wraps me in a thick, luxurious white towel. He already has his own wrapped around his waist, the fabric tenting from his erection.

I nod toward him. "Aren't you going to do something about that?" I don't know why I ask him that, perhaps because I'm fucking crazy.

He smirks and tilts his head. "Are you offering, little bird?"

I take a step back. "No."

His smirk drops. "Then no. I'm not a teenager. I don't masturbate."

My brow furrows. "Everyone masturbates."

"Not me." He licks his lips. "Do you masturbate, Alice?"

His voice is so serious you'd think we were discussing something mundane like the weather. Heat floods my cheeks, and I know I must be the color of a tomato. "I won't answer that."

He grabs my wrist and yanks me toward him. "Answer me." The lethal edge to his voice steals all the oxygen in the air.

"Yes," I murmur.

"Show me."

I freeze in shock. "W-What?"

"Show me how you do it." He nods to the bed. "Lie down and show me."

"No."

His brow furrows, and he looks irritated. "I don't like that word, little bird. *No* is a word that people don't say to me. Do you know why?" He grabs my throat, squeezing in a warning. "Because when I'm angry, I'm unstoppable." He releases my throat. "Do as you're told."

I feel self-conscious as I force my legs to move toward the bed, lying down before him.

And then I open my legs, sheer humiliation taking hold, as his eyes fix on my soaking wet pussy. The evidence of what this man does to me is as clear as day.

"Wet. So wet." His eyes flash. "Touch yourself."

I move my hand between my thighs and rub my clit, my back arching despite myself. The need I feel is unlike anything I've felt in a long time. It's desperate, and soon enough, I forget Taren's watching me like a hungry predator.

And all I can think about is him pinning me down to the bed and taking me against my will. The idea sends me higher, my nipples turning so hard they hurt. I plunge three fingers inside myself to quench the ache and finger fuck my pussy like a slut desperate for cock. And I imagine it's his cock, tearing me apart.

"Beautiful," he muses, drawing my attention back to him. "What's the part of you that responds to my touch but isn't touched itself? A place that hardens with desire yet remains unseen?"

I can hardly think, let alone respond to his riddles.

He watches me with the intensity of a predator, his gaze roaming over me as I lay bare before him. It feels like an eternity of silence follows before he speaks, "You're using it right now. I wonder what pretty, perverse images flash through that mind of yours. Tell me."

My lips fall open. "I don't know."

"Don't lie to me," he growls. "I want a detailed description of the fantasy flashing behind your eyelids when you shut them."

What the hell does it matter now?

I don't see any way out of this, so I push my pride aside. This man doesn't know me, and if I make it out alive, I'll never see him again. "I imagine you pinning me down and slamming your cock inside me while I scream *no*."

He recoils at that, eyes narrowing. "What darkness lives inside my pretty little bird?"

"I imagine you tearing me apart roughly while I tell you to stop, and all the while, I love every second."

He groans, squeezing his cock through his towel. "Naughty little Alice. You've got a dirty mind for such an innocent-looking bird."

I'm emboldened by his response. "I imagine you fucking my ass while I tell you to stop, too. I imagine you using every one of my holes." My hips rise off the bed as I get so close to shattering I know I won't last much longer.

"Good," he says roughly. His voice has lost the

careful control he had before. "I want you to come for me. Let me see you."

I slam my fingers in one last time, and that's enough. Stars dance behind my shut eyelids, and a gush of liquid squirts onto the bed.

"Fuck," he grunts, and I look up to see his towel is gone, and he's squeezing the base of his cock, but not stroking. "I bet you'd look so pretty with every hole gaping from my cock and cum dripping out of them. Such a pretty little bird, full of cum." And then he comes, shooting a thick rope onto the floor.

I moan, realizing at that moment how perverse this is. However, I've been drawn to the perverse for a while. And days stuck in a jail cell have brought that darkness to the forefront of my mind. There's something about this man that I can't seem to resist.

"Get up," he demands.

I stand for him, naked and ashamed.

He walks toward me and stops mere inches away, cupping my face and forcing me to look at him. "So beautiful," he breathes, his breath ghosting my skin. "Now it's time to dress you up."

I arch a brow. "I'm not a doll."

He chuckles. "No, but you need to look the part."

"The part for what?"

His expression turns cold. "No questions." He nods

71

toward a door. "Clothes are in there on the back of the door. Dress now."

A shiver races down my spine as I do as I'm told, feeling his gaze on me until I disappear into the walk-in closet. On the bench in the center is a set of luxurious lingerie. The bra, a demi-cup style, is made of black fabric with a panel that's entirely sheer at the top. The matching panties are in the same black fabric, and there's a garter belt, making me blush at the thought of wearing it. When I pick up the panties, I almost die as I realize they're crotchless.

Glancing at the back of the door, my heart skips a beat. A stunning dress is hanging on a golden hanger, which looks like it was spun from the moonlight. The soft and flowing fabric is a delicate shade of champagne, adorned with intricate hand-stitched patterns of silver thread. The dress's hourglass silhouette promises to flatter my figure and has a plunging neckline. In addition, there's a pair of matching stilettos with straps encrusted with crystals.

Why is this man letting me wear these clothes?

The part he'll have me play must have a sinister motive. I wish I wasn't so intrigued to find out what it is. Taren is the ultimate riddle that I'd love to learn the answer to.

8

TAREN

I sit opposite my temptress, focusing on the clouds passing by the window. Even as I try to ignore her, all I can think about is the way she spread her legs for me and made herself come.

Naughty Alice.

Dirty Alice.

She fantasized about me taking her against her will, and it took all my control not to give in and slam inside her, but I don't just want to fuck her. I want to possess her. Every tiny piece and fragment of her soul. Until I'm all she can think about. Until she can't breathe easily when I'm not near. Until her sole reason for living is me.

The purr of the jet's engines is the only sound that punctuates the silence. Other than a few unanswered questions about where I'm taking her, she's been quiet. We've been in the air for over an hour and have two to go.

"Sir, would you like a drink?" The hostess asks, batting her eyelashes, which are so fake they look hilarious.

I shake my head. "Alice, do you want anything?"

Alice glances at me before looking at the hostess. "Just water, please."

She nods and walks away to get Alice her water.

I meet Alice's gaze, and she looks irritated. "Not long now, and we'll be landing."

"Where exactly?"

I exhale a breath. "Mexico City." A shudder races through me. I can hardly believe she's sending me back there after all these years.

"Why?"

I sit forward with my hands before me, searching her sky-blue eyes. "The why isn't important. You're to play a part for me. That's all you need to know."

"What part?"

My jaw clenches. "You just need to be beautiful, like a swan."

Her brow furrows in confusion. "What's that supposed to mean?"

"You're going to help me at an event. Be pretty on my arm."

"And you couldn't have picked anyone else for that?"

I couldn't imagine anyone else by my side, ever. Alice is a true gem; I never want to be without her. "Could Hades have picked anyone but Persephone?"

She straightens, and her face turns pale. "Why are you holding me and my friends captive?"

I tilt my head. "Me? I'm not your captor, little bird."

"Who is?"

I smirk at the question. Alice is lucky she's yet to meet the woman who keeps her behind bars. "The Red Queen."

Her confusion deepens.

"You made a grave mistake coming on vacation to Puerto Nuevo. The northwest coast of Mexico is dangerous, and do you know why?"

She shakes her head.

"Because it's ruled by her. She's the darkness and pain. She brings blood and carnage wherever she goes." I clench my jaw as flashbacks try to surface, but I force them away, banishing them to far corners of my mind. "You, little bird, have flown into the jaws of Ileana Navarro."

Her face pales further. "The Navarro cartel?"

"Clever little bird." I lean back in my seat, watching her.

"And what does Ileana Navarro intend to do with us?"

A question I don't wish to answer. If Ileana had her way, the two vilest men in her employ would train them to be good, submissive slaves. Thiago and Matias are brothers. They say I'm mad, but those two are pure evil. Matias is a psychopath in the truest form. My madness is not my nature, but it's a part of me now.

"You don't want to know."

She swallows hard, her slender neck bobbing temptingly. What I'd do to see my bruises on her porcelain skin like a collar around her neck. "I'm going to die here, aren't I?"

I don't answer her question, but I sure as hell don't want my little bird to die. When I don't speak, I see tears forming in her eyes. A painful sensation ignites in the center of my chest. "Don't weep, little bird. Be strong."

She wipes a few tears from her face, shaking her head. "It's difficult when there's no hope."

"If hope has flown away. In a night, or in a day, In a vision, or in none, is it therefore the less gone? All that we see or seem is but a dream within a dream."

Her eyes widen at my Edgar Allan Poe quote. "You like poetry?" She asks.

My smile widens. "Clever, Alice. Yes, I do."

"Edgar Allan Poe is my favorite. What poem of his is your favorite?" She asks, surprising me. I'm not sure why she wants to know anything about me.

It's an easy choice for me. "The Raven is my favorite, but I enjoy most of his poetry. It's very..."

"Real?"

Tension coils through me. As people don't finish my sentences, most can't understand what I'm saying. I've never felt more exposed as I search Alice's sky-blue eyes. It's as if she can see past all my layers and right to the heart. "Real," I repeat the word and nod. "Yes."

She flushes, something she does far too much around me. It makes it difficult to hold myself back, but I have to. When I finally have my Alice beneath me, she will beg me to make her mine. Although, if she had it her way, she'd be begging me to stop while I fuck her senseless, while I take her against her will.

I wonder what darkness lurks within her pretty exterior. What I'd do to crack open her mind and see her hidden secrets.

"What are you thinking?" she asks.

People never ask me that. Normally, because they

BIANCA COLE

don't want to know what dark thoughts lurk in the corners of my tortured mind.

"I'm thinking I want to know what you're thinking," I respond, mirroring her question.

"You," she utters finally, her voice barely above a whisper. "I'm thinking about you."

"And what exactly about me are you thinking?"

Her cheeks flush again. "That I'd like to know more about you."

"And I, you, little bird." I clench my jaw. "Come here."

She stands and walks toward me, gasping as I grab her hand and lift her onto my lap, forcing her to straddle me. "Taren," she breathes my name.

"Alice," I tease.

Her eyes flicker shut, and her hips move softly, feeling the hardness of my erection beneath her. "Am I insane?"

"We're all mad here, little bird." I tease my hand up the front of her dress, knowing I picked well. She looks stunning. And then I wrap my hand around her throat, enjoying how it fits perfectly. As if they made this woman for me. "I'm mad to yearn for you."

Her sky-blue eyes open and meet mine. "Yearn for me?"

He nods. "Yes, with an intensity that threatens to

consume me," I murmur, my voice so low I can barely hear it over the hum of the engines. My fingers trace the curve of my little bird's throat. "The Red Queen watches and waits."

Her brow furrows in confusion. "What?"

I smile at her. "I'll reveal all in time."

My words irritate her as she exhales a deep breath. "You're the most confusing man I've ever met."

I grab her hips and squeeze. "And how many men have you met?" The dark vines of jealousy twist around my heart, weaving their way into my bloodstream. I don't want to think of Alice ever even talking to another man, no matter that it was before we met.

She wets her lips. "A few."

I grab her hair and yank it hard. "How many have been inside you?"

Her throat bobs, and tears fill her eyes, a few stray ones escaping down her cheek. "Two by choice."

"By choice?" I release her hair, cupping her chin. "And not by choice?"

She shakes her head, the tears coming faster now. "One," she breathes.

Red-hot, possessive anger floods me with an intensity that threatens to tear me apart. The thought of my bird being broken by someone against her will drives me insane. And they say I'm already fucking mad. What I'd give to bathe in his blood.

I growl, shaking my head. "Name."

Her eyes widen. "What?"

"Give me the bastard's name."

She shudders, her body so small and fragile on my lap. "Why?"

"Little bird, don't deny me. You won't like what happens if you do."

She bites her inner cheek. "His name is Michael Lovell." Her throat bobs. "He's a professor at the university I attend."

My brow furrows. "He still is?"

She nods. "Yes."

"Why the fuck isn't he in jail?"

She shakes her head, looking smaller by the second. "Because who would believe me if I told them?"

"Oh, little bird," I breathe. I shake my head, the vein in my temple throbbing with an anger that blazes like wildfire. "I'll make them believe," I promise. Some would say this is madness. To feel such over a woman I hardly know, but then I know her. My soul recognized her when we met, drew me to her, and entwined us.

I gently wipe away the tears that streak her face. "Michael Lovell won't escape justice."

Her gaze locks with mine, a mixture of fear and hope in her eyes. "Promise?" she whispers, her voice as delicate as a feather caught in a gale.

"Promise." My word is resolute, a vow carved in stone. When I next go Stateside, Michael Lovell won't breathe for long. "He'll pay."

Alice curls into me, her head on my chest, and I hold her.

Alice's head would be on a pike if Ileana could see me now. She can't stand the idea of losing me, not that she ever had me. Alice's arrival is going to force my hand.

I've got a queen to behead. And once she's dead, I have a professor's blood to bathe in.

9

ALICE

I'm in hell disguised as heaven.

As Taren leads me into the opulent penthouse suite and the fanciest hotel I've ever entered, I'm still trying to figure out why I'm here.

He needs arm candy. Surely, there were many women he could have picked. And yet, there was something odd about our conversation on the plane. I've no idea why I told him about Michael. It was a moment of insanity.

Not even my friends know what happened that night on campus.

My friends go on to me about my reluctance to date, but that's because they don't know why I'm scared to be intimate. They're oblivious to the horrifying truth about the night my professor violated my trust. He thrust me into an endless nightmare, leaving me scarred.

Since that night two years ago, I haven't had sex. And yet, I've had sick fantasies about being raped. None of it makes logical sense. I fear that when I have sex again, it won't be rough enough. Now, I'm broken, and the only way to feel is to be violated. Until Taren came along.

How he looks at me turns me on, and I realize that only cements the truth I've feared. I'm fucked in the head. Michael's treatment of me has screwed me up for good.

I'm broken.

Discardable.

"Why did you bring me?" I ask.

Taren looks at me briefly. "There's no other."

It's a half-answer, one that doesn't really make sense. There was no one else available? "My three best friends are all far more beautiful than me. You could have—"

He cuts me off with a savage snarl. "Say that again, and I'll put over my knee and spank you."

"It's the truth—"

He grabs my throat hard. "You, Alice, are the most beautiful thing I've ever seen. Your friends." He shakes his head. "None of them appealed to me. It was you." He grinds his teeth, eyes flashing with barely contained rage. "It was you I wanted by my side."

I swallow hard.

"Do you understand?"

Not exactly. I'll never understand how a man could pick me over my three best friends, but I'm glad he did. "Yes," I murmur.

"Good, now I never want to hear you put yourself down like that." His jaw clenches. "Fucking Michael has done a number on you, hasn't he?" He paces up and down, muttering under his breath in Spanish. I catch a few words, but my Spanish isn't the best.

"What do you mean?"

"He's broken you." He meets my gaze. "But don't worry little bird. I'll fix you." He clears his throat. "But right now, we've got to focus on tonight's event." Taren's eyes flit back to the tablet in his hands. "Come, sit." He slumps into the sofa, and I sit beside him, fiddling with my hands in my lap.

"The Estrada Cartel's leader, Pablo, will be in attendance." He brings up a picture of an older, balding man with a gray mustache. "This is him."

I nod. "Okay."

"Ileana believes he's trying to agree a deal to give him Mexico City. I don't believe it, but we must be her eyes and ears. Spies in plain sight. Blend in and look the part on my arm."

"Sounds easy enough."

He smiles at me. "Maybe. But we need to monitor these players, too. Javier Estrada, Lionel Estrada and Maria Estrada. All three will be in attendance, and we need to ensure none of them are working to secure Mexico City."

"What's so important about Mexico City?"

He chuckles. "Anyone who controls Mexico City controls the whole fucking country. It's the hub."

"Who controls it now?" I ask.

"No one. It's a free-for-all, and that's how it must stay."

Taren's words send a chill down my spine. The thought of being in the same room as these powerful and dangerous people makes me feel nauseous. I'm just a creative writing major at Brown University and completely out of my depth.

"They're going to know I don't belong," I breathe.

Taren shakes his head. "No, they won't." His eyes burn with confidence. "You belong because you believe you belong. And tonight, little bird, you'll wear that belief as your most glamorous attire."

I smile and nod.

If Luna, Blake, and Kali could see me now, they'd

wonder what the fuck I'm doing. Guilt floods me as I know they're locked in a cell while I'm planning to go to a fancy event with a madman. And I'm actually enjoying his company.

Why am I helping him so willingly?

Why did I tell him about the incident that has haunted me for two years?

He's the first person I've uttered the words to, and it's because, despite how utterly unbelievable it is, I trust him. I trust him, and I don't know why. It's as if he sees the real me like no one else ever has.

"So, what now?" I ask, glancing at the clock on the wall. It's only three in the afternoon, and the event isn't until tonight.

Taren stands up, the couch's leather creaking under his movement, and extends his hand to me. "Let's take a walk," he suggests, his eyes gleaming with anticipation. "The streets of Mexico City are a narrative, a visual story of the past, the struggles, and the spirit of the people who call this city their home." He speaks as though from experience, and I wonder if he called Mexico City home once before.

"You know the city well?" I ask.

His jaw clenches. "Unfortunately."

I nod. "Okay, a walk."

Stepping out of the luxurious confines of the hotel,

the world transforms into a vivid tableau of life and color. The buildings are painted in a kaleidoscope of colors. Street vendors peddle their wares, offering a sensory overload of flavors, sights, and sounds while children chase each other around the bustling squares.

"This city feels alive," I say.

Taren glances at me. "It always has." His jaw clenches. "I want to show you something."

"What?" I ask.

"You'll see," he replies, tightening his grasp on my hand and yanking me away from the crowds. My stomach twists a little as we walk through a quieter part of the city, with derelict houses and beggars on every corner.

Taren pulls me gently down a narrow street. At the end of the road stands what I can only describe as a relic of what once was a house. The walls look like a bomb has blasted them, reduced to a skeletal frame with jagged chunks of concrete. The roof is non-existent, swallowed by the ravages of time as weeds and trees grow out of the top. Its windows, empty sockets, stare blankly at us as if harboring a thousand untold stories of hardship.

"This," Taren says, barely above a whisper, "is where I was born."

My chest clenches as I stare at the rubble of his childhood. "What happened?"

"It's not important." He glances at me, his eyes unreadable. "It's nothing but rubble, ash, and weeds watered with blood."

Blood.

I struggle to imagine what kind of carnage Taren witnessed here. I reach out to touch his arm, my heart aching for him. "I'm sorry, Taren," I whisper.

His entire body tenses. "There's nothing to be sorry for."

"How old were you when this happened?" I ask to learn more about what made him the way he is.

"Eight." He doesn't look at me, staring at the house blankly.

"Did your family die?" I ask, wondering how many parallels can be drawn between us. I was eight when my birth parents and sister died in a car accident. "My birth parents died when I was eight. And my sister," I blurt out.

His jaw clenches and he glances at me, nostrils flaring. "What did you say?"

I don't know why I blurted that out. "My parents died when I was eight along with my two year old sister in a car accident."

He stares at me for a few beats, before turning his

gaze back to the skeletal remains of the house. "I never was, but always will be. No one ever saw me, but everyone will. What am I?"

I realize he won't answer my question as to whether his family died. This man is an enigma. He brings me to his childhood home, and yet he's not willing to open up about what happened. And why would he? We barely know each other.

"Death," I breathe.

He nods in response, a jarring smile considering where we are. "Clever little bird."

A shiver races down my spine. This man can be as changeable as the wind. While he tells me he wants to save me from his boss, I sense he can be cruel. That danger follows him like a shadow, and I need to be careful not to be drawn into his web of madness.

"Why did you bring me here?" I demand.

He glances back at the rubble with an odd expression. "To show you my beginning." He turns to look at me. "To let you see the ashes from which I rose, the desolation that forged me." He tilts his head. "I needed you to see this, understand where I come from, and understand me."

I shake my head. "I don't know if I'll ever understand you, Taren."

His eyes flash with irritation, and his jaw clenches. "Why not?"

I place my hand on his chest gently. "Because you're the most complicated riddle I've ever encountered."

He smirks, a hint of madness shining in his dark, onyx eyes. "Good, but you want to solve me, don't you, little bird?"

The crazy thing is my answer to that question is yes. I want to solve him. I know I shouldn't because he's dangerous. And he may not be the man responsible for holding me captive, but he works for the person who is responsible.

"Yes," I breathe.

His smirk widens and my heart rate stutters as I realize telling him that is dangerous. Now he knows the power he holds over me. And I fear that's the most dangerous thing of all.

10

TAREN

*T*he event is in full swing when we arrive.

Alice clutches me like I'm her crutch. I'd love to be that for her. I want to be her entire world. I want the rest of the world to burn until it's only us left in it. The rightful king and queen.

And so the spectacle unfolds.

Mexico City hasn't been the devil I expected. Perhaps my little bird helps keep the violent onslaught of my memories at bay. I'm unsure. However, I expected to feel chaotic and out of control. All I know is I breathe easier with her close. As if she's my oxygen. As if she's my salvation.

A twisted and maddening obsession has taken hold of me. I force myself to stop thinking of the woman by my side and focus on the plan. The room is full of people who act like marionettes being pulled by the invisible strings of social obligation.

Most of the laughter and chatter that fills the room sounds fake. And their eyes are empty and soulless. Such is Mexico City.

Alice is different in every way. She's a jewel in the darkness. A beacon of light in this cesspit that is Mexico City. I watch her, drinking in every little thing about her.

"There he is," Alice murmurs, her eyes fixed on Pablo Estrada.

She learns quick. I'm so distracted by her that I might have to rely on her to do my job. Which means I need to get a handle on myself.

"Well done."

She smiles at me. "A drink?" she suggests.

"Good idea."

Pablo stands by the bar, so it makes sense for us to get a drink.

I keep hold of Alice's hand and lead her to the bar. The noise and chatter fade away as we get closer to Pablo. He shouldn't recognize me, as I haven't met him, and Ileana has been careful to ensure I kept my face out of the media because I'm her spymaster. Pablo turns, and his dark eyes brush over us with disinterest as we sit on two free stools at the bar a few feet from him.

I let out a breath I didn't know I was holding, leaning toward Alice. "We're in the clear."

She relaxes slightly.

"What can I get for you?" the bartender asks.

"Scotch on the rocks." I glance at Alice, realizing I don't know what she drinks. I know nothing about her, but I want to know it all. "What would you like, baby?"

The nickname baby is for the show here at the event, but her eyes flash, and her nostrils flare as if it affects her. "A margarita, please."

The bartender smiles. "Coming up."

I tap my fingers against the hardwood bar, listening as Pablo speaks with the city commissioner.

"How much will it cost?" Pablo asks.

The commissioner glances around the room to check no one's listening, and I move to kiss Alice on the cheek as if I'm engrossed in my girl.

She shudders at my light touch. "What was that for?"

I lean close to her ear. "Cover. They can't suspect us."

"Right," she murmurs, her eyes fixed on my lips as

if willing me to kiss her again. "If you keep doing that, I'll forget why we're here."

I chuckle. "Focus, little bird."

"I'm trying," she murmurs, clutching onto my hand as if her life depends on it. "Can you hear what he's saying?"

I kiss her cheek again. "When you're quiet, yes." And then I press my lips to her mouth for the first time.

She tenses before relaxing into it. Her mouth parting for me while I try to listen to the conversation behind us. My mind is too drawn to the woman in my arms. Her taste is as sweet as I remember, and I want to lose myself. Control snaps the whip in my mind, and I force myself away, straightening up. "We shouldn't do that again, or I'll lose focus."

Alice is flushed, and her lips swollen from the kiss. "Right." She tugs her bottom lip between her teeth, testing my self-control.

I chuckle. "Don't do that, little bird."

Her wide eyes meet mine, and I can see the hunger there, mirroring mine. It's dangerous, this game we're playing. I came here on a mission for Ileana, but Alice could be my downfall.

"We need to focus," I murmur.

Her eyes remain on my lips when the bartender

returns, placing her margarita on the counter. She turns toward him, breaking the spell. "Thank you."

"And one scotch on the rocks," the bartender says. "Cash or card?"

I pass him my card, and he swipes it. "Thanks. Have a good evening." I take my card and drink before guiding Alice away from the bar but still within listening distance from Pablo and the commissioner.

"Can you understand what they're saying?"

I turn her around so her back is to the two men and carefully glance at them to read their lips. "They're definitely discussing him agreeing a deal. What for, I'm not sure..."

Alice's lips purse together. "How are we supposed to learn why he's here?"

"We listen, watch, and wait. Little bird." I lean toward her and kiss her cheek softly. "Have patience."

She shivers at my touch. "Okay, shall we look for the other Estradas?" She asks.

I nod, loving how quickly she picks up how this works. It's like she fits into this world by my side. The only problem is Ileana is still a fucking obstacle.

"We should mingle," I suggest, watching Alice nod in agreement. We begin to navigate the sea of people, pretending to be another couple caught up in the glittering event. Suddenly, Javier Estrada approaches us, his dark eyes scrutinizing.

"Hello," he says, a predatory smile forming. "I don't believe we've met."

"I'm Enrique," I tell him, pulling Alice closer. Assuming a fake identity. There's no way I can let them know that I'm from the Navarro Cartel. "And this is my girlfriend, Alice."

"A pleasure, Enrique, Alice," Javier says, his gaze lingering uncomfortably on Alice. I feel a fierce protectiveness surge, tightening my grip around her. "You're new in town?"

"We've been here a while, actually," I lie smoothly, my eyes never leaving his. "Just been keeping a low profile, enjoying each other's company."

"Of course," Javier chuckles, though a glint in his eye suggests he's not buying it. "Well, enjoy your evening."

As Javier walks away, Alice lets out a shaky breath. "That was intense," she murmurs, looking at me.

"We survived," I reply, a half-smile playing on my lips. "Now, let's keep doing what we're here for."

We blend into the crowd, with Alice staying close to my side. As we're passing by a quiet corner, I hear the familiar voice of Maria Estrada, her words carried over in hushed tones.

I yank Alice against me and bring my lips to her ear. "Quiet, little bird. Act like we're wrapped up in each other."

She places her hand tentatively on my chest. Right above my heart as it thuds erratically.

"Lionel, securing the mayor's favor is crucial if we're going to secure Mexico City and the whole of Mexico," Maria's voice is insistent, a touch of urgency in her tone. "It's the only way we can broker this deal. We need him on our side."

"Si, Maria, I know," Lionel replies. "I've already started buttering him up. Invited him for dinner next week."

"Good. Remember, Lionel, we can't afford any mistakes," Maria continues. "Pablo's expecting us to get this sorted. This is bigger than us. It's about legacy."

I glance at Alice, her eyes wide as she processes the information. My little bird knows what that means. It means Ileana's suspicions were right. The question is, how will I use this information to my advantage?

I sweep Alice away from the corner and wrap a possessive arm around her waist. "Dance with me," I demand.

Her eyebrows raise a little. "What?"

"I said, dance with me," I breathe, my lips ghosting

her cheek. "It's a demand, not a question, in case you were wondering."

She nods in response as I pull her onto the dance floor in the middle of the ballroom.

My fingers trace the curve of Alice's waist, my grip tightening. The sensuous strains of a tango meet our ears. I guide her through the moves, and it's clear she's danced before. Either that, or she's a natural. That thought angers me, though. I don't want to think of her dancing with anyone but me. She's mine.

The music is intoxicating. My heart hammers like a blacksmith's anvil, forging love and madness equally.

I move my hands lower to her hips, and she shudders, making me smirk. "My little bird, how you flutter under my touch," I muse. "Does it terrify you, the darkness within me? Or does it call to you?"

She swallows, and her slender throat bobs, drawing all my attention to it. I want to wrap my hands around her neck and choke her while she comes on my cock. The dirty thoughts I have about my little Alice are uncharacteristic.

"Answer me," I command.

She shrugs. "Both," she barely whispers.

Her answer pleases me. I want her fear and her intrigue. I want every fucking emotion she can feel. And I want her to experience them with me. To learn what it is to truly open your soul to another. "Will you break for me, little bird?"

Her brow furrows. "What do you mean?"

I lean toward her ear. "I want you broken and mine. I want to fit all your broken pieces against mine until we make one whole piece."

She shudders. "I was broken before we met."

My jaw clenches. "By Michael?" I confirm the dark tone of my voice audible.

"Perhaps, but I think I was broken before," She breathes.

"We're all broken from the start. Like jagged puzzle pieces searching for the missing pieces," I whisper.

She looks at me, those enchanting sky-blue eyes wide with something akin to apprehension, fascination, and something else I can't quite place. "What if we're beyond repair?" She questions, her voice barely audible over the music.

"I don't want to repair you, little bird. I want to reshape you," I reply.

She looks confused. "I don't understand."

The music dies down as we sway to the last few notes. "What is more beautiful for having been broken?"

She bites her lip. "I'm not very good at these."

I chuckle. "You'll get better. It's a mosaic." I pull her

off the dance floor. "Broken pieces put together to create a masterpiece. There's beauty in the broken." I pull her toward the exit of the ballroom. "Now, we've got what we came for. Let's leave."

I've got no intention of remaining in such a dangerous place for longer than necessary, especially with my treasure by my side. We've made an appearance and got what we came here for. The information. The question is whether I give it to Ileana or not.

Alex, the man she sent with us, hasn't even bothered to make an appearance. No doubt too drunk in strip clubs already. It suits me though. Because it means the information learned tonight is mine to do with as I please.

Taking Ileana down is my main objective. And this useful information could be one of the puzzle pieces in orchestrating her downfall.

11
ALICE

There's a tension in the air as we enter the hotel room. Another man came with us and is supposed to be staying in the bedroom opposite, but there's no one in the suite. I wonder if Taren will touch me tonight. The huge penthouse suite has two bedrooms and a pullout bed in the living area too, so we don't have to share.

Is it fucked up that I want to share with him?

Probably.

"Bedroom," Taren orders.

I clear my throat, looking into those dark, allusive eyes. They're unreadable, as always. "Okay." I walk toward the bedroom and hear his brogues squeaking on the oak floor as he follows me. Goosebumps rise over every inch of my body. My nipples tighten, and I'm wet from the anticipation.

"Strip, little bird."

I turn to face him, my lips pursing. "Why?"

"You can't sleep in that dress. It's worth ten thousand dollars."

My eyes widen. "You're joking."

He shakes his head. "No."

I carefully slip it off, placing it on a chair nearby. When I turn around, Taren's eyes are alight with pure fire. They drag down my body predatory and then back up slowly.

"In bed."

I swallow hard at the edge of his tone. "What are you going to do to me?"

His jaw clenches. "In bed," he repeats.

I climb into the bed, and he strips off, revealing his corded muscles covered in ink and scars. I melt at the sight of him. When I see him like that, I'm pretty sure he could do whatever the fuck he wanted to me.

Taren crosses the room, his muscular form a daunting silhouette against the hotel suite's softly lit backdrop. He slides into the bed next to me, an electric current buzzing between us despite the distance he maintains. He settles in, his tattooed arm folded behind his head as he stares at the ceiling.

"Sleep," he commands, his voice firm.

His word, simple as it may be, wreaks havoc with my mind. The anticipation, the uncertainty, it's maddening. A thousand questions whir in my mind, but the silence in the room is deafening, punctuated only by the distant hum of the city outside.

"That's it?" I blurt out.

He raises a brow but keeps staring at the ceiling, the whisper of a smirk on his lips. "What were you expecting, little bird?" He turns, and his piercing gaze catches mine, stealing the oxygen from my lungs. "Did you want me to violate you?" His eyes narrow and it feels like a taunt to what I told him earlier.

"Hey, that's not fair."

His jaw clenches. "You told me the truth about Michael. It confuses me. Especially after what you told me you fantasized about in my bedroom before we left." He reaches out, dragging a finger across the swell of my breasts. "Make me understand."

I shut my eyes hard. "I can't because I don't understand."

"I'm not judging you, little bird." His voice is reassuring, and I open my eyelids, looking into his coffee-colored eyes and wishing I could explain it. "I want to understand you. All of you."

Silence passes before I gather my thoughts, my

heart pounding against my chest. "I don't know," I admit, my voice barely above a whisper. "A part of me is drawn to you, to the danger and excitement. But there's another terrified part that remembers what happened with Michael." I pause, my eyes darting to his, searching for any sign of judgment and finding none. "It feels like if I act it out, and it's my choice with you, then it'll give me power over the situation." I shake my head. "It makes no sense. I know."

Taren remains silent, his gaze never leaving mine. He reaches out, tugging a loose strand of my hair behind my ear, his touch causing my breath to hitch. "That's honest," he murmurs, his voice soft in the dim light. "Such a good little bird."

"Can you be honest with me?" I ask, biting my lip.

He nods.

"What's going to happen to me and my friends?"

His jaw clenches. "Nothing, I hope."

I arch a brow. "How's that possible?"

"I have a plan." He puts his arm behind his head again, gazing at the ceiling. "The details aren't important. The plan has been on the sidelines for a long time, but your arrival has made its execution imperative."

"But in the meantime, what's our fate?" I push.

He turns again, looking at me. "Training to be sex slaves."

I tense, my heart pounding erratically against my rib cage. "What?"

"Your training starts tomorrow. And I'm sorry, but I can't stop it. If I'm going to get you and your friends out, she can't know of our... connection."

I don't dare ask what the training entails.

"Have hope, little bird." He leans over, kissing me. "I won't let them hurt you if I can help it."

"Who's Ileana to you?"

He stiffens and pulls back, shaking his head. "That's a very complicated question." It's like walls shut down over his eyes. "Sleep," he says.

I don't want to sleep, though. Something tells me that this spell will break from tomorrow, and hell will ensue. I need to feel at least for tonight.

"No," I breathe.

Taren's brow furrows as I move to straddle him, leaning down to kiss his lips. At first, he stiffens before grabbing my hips and deepening the kiss, his tongue thrusting into my mouth.

"If hell is waiting for me, I want to remain in heaven a little longer," I say.

He groans as I roll my hips, grinding against his

thick erection. "Naughty Alice. The problem is, I'm the devil, so this can't be heaven."

I shake my head. "You're not my devil. You're my God," I murmur.

He growls, biting my lip. "That's right, baby. And I'll rule you." He flips me over, his strong, powerful body pinning me to the bed. "If you need me to stop, tell me." His eyes flash with barely contained control.

I shake my head. "Never."

He kisses me passionately, his hands gripping my hips hard. "Alice," he breathes my name before trailing his lips down the curve of my neck.

I moan, sliding my fingers through his dark hair. "I need you."

He pulls back and searches my eyes. "Not yet, baby. Not tonight."

I groan. Hearing this man call me baby is so intoxicating.

What the hell would Luna say if she could see me now?

I can imagine her berating me for turning down all her attempts to set me up while falling into bed with a fucking madman who works for the woman who kidnapped us. And yet, I know the source of this dark desire. It's something I'll never understand. Why being taken advantage of by someone I trusted has twisted me up.

Taren is someone I should fear, and instead, I desire him. I desire him like I've desired no man for two years. This desire feels stronger than any I've felt before the incident.

"Please," I beg against his lips, arching my back as his heavy cock presses against my center.

He nips at my collarbone with his teeth. "I said not tonight," he groans. "You'll need to wait for my cock, but I'll taste your sweetness, little bird."

I moan as he kisses a path down my stomach, heading toward my panties. My body is on fire. His touch drives me insane. And when he gets down there, he tears my panties in two like an animal, even though there was no need since they're crotchless.

"So wet for me, little bird." His breath ghosts over my clit, setting my nerve ending on fire. "Are you turned on?" he asks.

"More than you'll ever know," I answer, biting down a moan as his tongue sweeps up my center. A wave of pleasure surges through me, setting every nerve on edge. "Taren, please," I breathe, my fingers tangling in his dark hair again.

He smirks, his eyes burning as they meet mine, filled with a dangerous promise. "Patience," he murmurs, the pad of his thumb making lazy circles over my throbbing clit, but never quite touching it. "We've got all night," Taren whispers.

I whimper at the thought of him teasing me to tears all night. "Please, I need to feel you—"

He sucks on my clit, breaking my sentence off halfway through.

"Fuck!" I breathe.

"You're one needy little bird, aren't you?" Taren taunts, his voice a low growl that vibrates against my sensitive skin.

He returns his thumb just above my clit and circles it softly. "I intend to memorize your body. And work out exactly how to make you tick tonight. You're the only puzzle I want to crack."

"That sounds like torture," I murmur.

"Torture can be a form of pleasure," Taren answers, a wild gleam in his eyes. His tongue traces the outline of my lower lips, eliciting a deep, guttural moan from me. "Remember, Alice, pleasure and pain are two sides of the same coin."

His warm breath brushes against my thigh as he chuckles. "You're scared, aren't you?" he whispers, his fingers trailing over my thighs.

"I'm not scared of you, Taren," I murmur, my voice a hoarse whisper.

"Good," he says, his voice a gravelly purr. "Because,

Alice, I'm about to make you feel things you've never imagined. I'm about to tear down your walls and taste the madness within." His words are a thrilling promise that sends shivers down my spine. I'm his to ruin, to rebuild, to set aflame. With Taren, I'm unbound.

The grin on Taren's face widens as he slides a finger inside me, inch by agonizing inch. He's watching me, studying my reactions, drinking in every gasp and whimper that escapes my lips. It's frustratingly slow.

Every nerve ending in my body is on fire, screaming for more. "Taren," I gasp, my back arching off the bed as he thrusts his finger deep inside. Yet, it's not enough, far from it. "Please," I gasp.

"Still not enough?" he asks. The dark glint in his eyes is cruel. He knows the wild craving he's ignited inside me.

I grind my teeth. "You're driving me crazy."

"Good," he replies, eyes flashing. "I want you as fucking mad as they call me. I want you to be driven to the brink the way you drive me to the fucking brink."

"Please," I beg, feeling no shame. I'm too desperate to feel. I'm too desperate for him to claw me out of the hole I've been in for two years. "I need you to make me feel again."

His eyes narrow. "What do you mean, again?"

I bite the inside of my cheek. "Since Michael, I..."

He growls at the mention of the professor who raped me. "Don't fucking say his name again. I'll deal with him, but I can't right now." He clenches his fists. "Are you saying you haven't been with a man since?"

I nod in response.

"Did he break my pretty bird's wings?" His voice is low, a barely controlled snarl.

Taren's words hang heavy in the air, a hurricane of wrath and protectiveness. Normally filled with madness, his eyes are now unmistakably dark with fury.

I'm about to speak when he shakes his head. "Quiet. I'll give you what you want." And then he devours me, my entire body turning to flames. He licks and sucks at my clit like a feral beast.

I moan as he eradicates all thoughts of the past the moment I feel him between my thighs. His teeth sink into my inner thigh as he slams two fingers deep inside me. "You're so fucking beautiful." He pulls back, lazily pushing his fingers in and out of me. "Possession isn't always about holding on tight. Sometimes, it's about the fall."

I don't know what he's talking about. All I know is his madness is as alluring as the rest of him.

"It's in that fall where we truly possess each other.

In the descent's chaos, I find you. In the splintering of control, you find me. We're each other's madness, the sweetest form of possession."

"In plain English?" I ask.

"You're mine," he breathes, dark eyes flashing as they find mine. "And I'm yours."

I shudder as it doesn't make sense. We don't know each other, yet my soul and every part of who I am agrees. As if we're two pieces of one whole that was broken apart and need to come back together.

And then he continues, sucking my clit into his mouth and making my back arch. It's as if he can read my body like a book. Every thing that feels good, he does repeatedly, so in tune with my pleasure.

Before I know it, I'm on the edge of an explosion. "Taren, I'm going to—"

"That's right. Come for me. I want you to shatter for me. Let me drown in your pleasure." His fingers hit a spot inside me that has my eyes rolling back in my head, and I can't help but cry out. "That's it," he urges, "let yourself fall into the madness. It's where we belong, you and I." The urgency in his voice is mirrored in his actions, his fingers and mouth working in overdrive, pushing me closer and closer to the edge.

And then I shatter for him. "Oh my God!" I scream.

My orgasm sets every nerve ending on fire. It's the most intense sensation I've ever experienced, making my body convulse.

"Damn it, your pussy is clenching my fingers so fucking hard, little bird." He groans, rubbing a hand across the bulge at his crotch. "My cock wants to be so fucking far inside you right now."

"Then fuck me," I breathe.

He smirks, shaking his head. "No, I told you. Not yet. Not tonight."

I grunt in frustration as he moves to the side, lying on the bed beside me before pulling my body against his chest. "Why not?" I ask.

His fingers move in soothing circles over my shoulder. "Because when I claim you. You'll want me so badly you'll be mad with desire and something deeper."

"I don't understand why you want me," I murmur.

"Why do I want you?" He chuckles. "Isn't it obvious? You're a flame in the darkness, a beacon of chaotic beauty in a world of monotonous order. And damn, it's intoxicating."

My heart flutters at his words, hating that I want him in ways I've never wanted anyone. I must be careful because I can already feel him sinking his claws into my heart. Taren doesn't strike me as a man who does love. He does obsession, possession, consuming madness. And that's what he wants, to consume me in his madness.

Is it crazy that I want him to?

12
TAREN

*R*eality is an incessant drizzle of disappointments and frustrations that taint our existence. I could have spent the rest of my life wrapped in Alice in Mexico City if I didn't know that Ileana would hunt me down.

Thinking of the devil, she sits before me, ignoring me despite sending someone to fetch me the moment the car stopped on the drive.

First, I returned Alice to her cell to ensure she was safe and with her friends. All of whom looked relieved to see her alive and well. And then I raced up here only for the Red Queen to ignore me like I'm nothing.

She finishes writing in her book and drops the pen, glancing at me with disinterest.

It begs the question of why she sent me to Mexico

City if she's so disinterested in what happened. I'm still torn on how much information to give her. It could be a powerful weapon in my arsenal. Giving her tidbits will keep her suspicion alive, but not confirmed.

The Estrada Cartel may be the answer to my problems. I will need an ally before this is over.

Staring into her dark, soulless eyes, I have visions of wrapping my hands around her throat and squeezing until the light drains from them, but I push the visions away. They're not an accurate representation of what's to come. When I kill the red queen, it'll be drawn out, painful, and bloody. Exactly how Michael Lovett will die, too. My plan needs to be flawless, and it's so close I can practically taste her blood tinging the air.

"Any news from the event?"

"I overheard him discussing purchasing real estate with the city commissioner. It's possible that your hunch was right." I shrug. "But there was no solid evidence of a plan," I lie.

"I knew it." She clenches her fists on the desk. "I need Pablo Estrada's head on a plate."

"That won't be easy." I keep my hands clasped in my lap. "He's as well guarded as you."

She arches a brow. "How well guarded?"

I spotted at least ten Estrada security guards at the event, none more than a yard from him. "Very well guarded."

"Tell me?" she demands.

"Ten guards at least at the event, all for him," I confirm.

"Chingada madre," she curses in Spanish. "We need to think of something, or he'll block our supply from the south. Anyone who controls Mexico City controls Mexico."

"I know." A part of me hopes he secures the deal, cutting her off at the heels. It would make my plan easier. So, I'm not ruling out approaching them, but the problem is getting the Estrada Cartel to trust me. "What do you propose?"

"We go to war," she announces as if she ordered a Taco.

Typical Ileana. The echoes of bloodshed and war resonate through her very being, intertwining with her existence. Wherever she goes, chaos follows.

"Are you sure that's a good idea? We don't know if he's working on a deal to secure the city."

"Why wouldn't it be a good idea?" Her eyes narrow. "His attempt on Mexico City is a declaration of war. I wonder what the Vasquez Cartel would think about it?" She drums her fingers on the desk before standing and walking toward the window behind her desk. "Call Damien Vasquez and invite him here."

I'm surprised to hear her willing to side with another cartel. She's not one for being cooperative, making me wonder what her motives are. "You want Damien to come here? Do you think he would accept?"

She glances over her shoulder at me. "Or a meeting at a location of his choosing. Just get it done."

I nod in response. "Of course. Is that all?" I ask.

She nods. "Yes, you can leave."

I stand and turn to leave.

"Wait, Taren." I turn to face her. "Give your mother a kiss."

A shudder travels through me. *Mother.* She's not a mother, and the idea of going that close to her willingly makes my skin crawl. A mother doesn't treat their son like she has treated me all these years. It's sick the things she'd done to me.

However, I force my reluctance away and numbly walk toward her, kissing her cheek. She grabs my hair and kisses me on the mouth, making vomit rise in my throat. Her constant blurring of the lines between us has always made me feel sick since I was old enough to understand it, but it feels even more disgusting after kissing Alice.

My salvation.

My light.

My little bird.

"You seem distracted."

I shake my head. "Not at all. I'm tired from traveling."

She looks irritated but nods. "Fine, get some rest."

I walk toward the door.

"Taren."

"Yes?" I ask, not looking back at her.

"Did you enjoy your prisoner?"

A shiver races down my spine. "The prisoner helped me blend in if that's what you mean."

She laughs, and it's callous and cruel. "Don't pretend you didn't fuck her. I don't care if you did. Just know she'll be entering training tomorrow. At least you warmed her up."

I don't physically react to her taunts. "And I'll be training her."

"What?" she asks, eyes flashing with anger.

"I'm bored, as I told you. I intend to have some fun with the prisoners." I glare back at her. "Do you have a problem with that, *Mother?*"

Her eyes narrow, but she shakes her head. "Of course not."

I walk away without another word. The risk of

insisting I'd help with training was high, but I've got no other way to keep Alice safe. I must always be present to keep the hungry wolves at bay.

Ileana can't learn the truth about Alice, or she'll tear her from me. Ileana is my nightmare. And it's almost time for me to wake up.

13

ALICE

"Oh my God!" Luna rushes toward me and wraps me in a tight hug, a sob tearing from her lips. "I thought you were dead. When I woke and…" She trails off, looking at me and checking me for any injuries. "What happened?"

A complicated question with no easy answer.

Guilt overwhelms me as I'm glad to see Luna but not to be locked in a cage again. Taren brought me back down here quickly after a man called Matias told him Ileana needed to see him immediately.

He locked me in and didn't say a word before leaving.

"It was weird." I slump down on the hay in the corner. "I don't know how to explain it." When I glance up, Luna looks at me with a concerned expression.

"Are you okay?"

I nod. "Yeah, it's just that Taren is so confusing."

She raises a brow. "Taren? You're on first-name terms with our kidnapper?"

Heat flows through my veins as I'm on more than first-name terms with him. Memories of how he made me beg yesterday in the hotel room flood my mind.

"Yeah, well... it's a long story." I avoid her gaze. "But he's not actually the guy holding us captive. It's his boss."

I've never felt more confused. I should hate Taren because he works for the woman who dragged us into this hell, but something tells me there's so much more to his story. His touch is electrifying, his kisses addictive, and the way he looks at me, it's like I'm the only person who exists in the world.

"Well, I think we have time to kill. Spill," Luna says.

I told Taren I'd keep our plan secret. My friends can't know he's trying to break us out of here because he's obsessed with me. I don't know how I'd explain that to them anyway.

Hey, guys. Our kidnapper wants to fuck me, so he's going to get us out, and I want to fuck him too...

I sense that wouldn't go down so well. It's crazy, but it's true. I've never had a connection like I have with Taren with anyone before.

"Is that Alice?" Blake's voice comes from the crack in the wall, giving me more time to develop a story.

"Yes, she's back," Luna says.

I walk toward the crack. "I'm okay."

Blake breathes a long sigh of relief. "Thank God for that."

"We thought the worst for a moment there," Kali says, her voice a little hoarse as she appears at the gaping crack between the two cells.

"Don't worry. I'm fine."

"What happened?" Blake asks.

"It was weird, if I'm honest." I sigh. "That guy, Taren, took me to Mexico City."

"What the hell for?" Luna asks.

"I had to pose as his date at an event he was under-cover at." I shrug.

"He didn't, you know…" Kali trails off.

I feel more heat flooding through my veins. "No."

But I wanted him to. It's fucked up, but it's the truth. I wanted Taren more than I've ever wanted a man. And certainly more than I've wanted a man in the last two years.

"Why are you blushing?" Blake asks, eyes narrowing.

I shrug. "I may have had to kiss him a few times, posing as his girlfriend. And he's not exactly bad looking, is all."

"Oh my God!" Luna exclaims, shaking her head. "You've got a serious case of Stockholm syndrome."

I roll my eyes. "Don't be so dramatic. I don't have Stockholm syndrome."

Blake clears her throat. "Not going to lie, Al, but you sound like you do."

I grind my teeth. Maybe I do have Stockholm Syndrome. But I doubt it. Stockholm Syndrome normally takes time to develop. The moment I locked eyes with Taren, I felt something deep. A shift I can't explain. "Whatever. The point is we're in for a shitty fucking experience."

Luna swallows. "What do you mean?"

I know that telling my friends about our training will freak them out, but at least it's better than leaving them to find out on their own. "Apparently, they're going to train us as sex slaves." I pause when both Blake and Luna gasp. "And then sell us to the highest bidder."

"Fuck," Luna says.

Kali clears her throat. "Do you know who has us?"

"The Navarro Cartel."

"Shit," Luna says, running a hand through her hair. "You don't reckon they'd reconsider if I sold them my hacking services, do you?" She shrugs. "I mean, I'm one of the best hackers in North America, even though I don't do that anymore since I almost got caught."

Luna spent her high school years taking jobs to hack into organizations and even the government. She made a lot of money, which she stashed in off-shore accounts, some of which she had to use to pay her college tuition after her parents found out and kicked her out of the house. The rest, she won't touch for fear it will get tracked. She's good. But I'm unsure how she'd broach that subject with the men who will train us.

"I doubt it, Luna. They probably make more money from us as sex slaves," Blake says.

Luna crosses her arms over her chest, looking determined. "No, I could bring them endless money if it's about that. I'm going to suggest it. What's the harm?"

I swallow hard. Taren would consider it, but what about Ileana?

"These people are dangerous. They'd murder you without a second thought," Kali says, her eyes wide with fear. "That's the harm."

"Kali's right. Even if they agreed, why would they let all four of us go? Surely it would just be you, Luna," I say.

Luna shakes her head. "I'd demand they let us all go if they want me to hack for them."

I sigh heavily. "Something tells me you can't make demands of the Navarro Cartel."

"Agreed," Blake says.

Kali nods. "I'm sorry, Luna, but I agree with them. It might put you in more danger than we're in now."

Luna sighs heavily and walks over to the hay in the cell's corner, dropping onto it. "I can't believe we're in this shit all because we wanted a cheap holiday." She rests her forehead on her forearms.

I can. I should have trusted my gut.

When Kali suggested the resort, I knew it was a dangerous area. I even told the three of them it was risky, but they wouldn't listen.

I glance through the gaping crack in the wall at my two other friends. "I guess we just have to wait now."

Blake and Kali nod as I go to sit with Luna on the hay. I place a hand on her shoulder and squeeze. "We'll find a way out of here. I'm sure of it."

Luna looks at me. "Do you realize what kind of shit they're going to put us through?"

I shake my head. "No, not exactly."

Luna shudders. "I hacked for a guy who wanted to take down a North American sex ring that was selling girls. And let's just say some of the shit I found was sicker than you could ever imagine."

"Like what?" I ask.

"Rape, necrophilia, cannibalism, somnophilia, and more. You name the sickest thing you can think of, and I've seen it."

The horror of what awaits us feels jarring compared to my thirty-six hours spent with Taren. My heart wants to believe that he can get us out. That somehow we'll make it through this. Because the alternative is too fucked up to dwell on.

She's right.

Men that buy women from the Cartel are going to be sick fuckers. For a start, they think it's okay to buy women, and that's all we need to know to work out the type of men they are.

"At least we've got each other," I murmur.

Her throat bobs as she looks at me. "For how long? I doubt the same man will buy all four of us. We might all end up in separate corners of the country. Hell, maybe different countries. Who knows?"

"My mom will lose her shit since she hasn't heard from me," I say.

Luna shrugs. "At least I don't have anyone that gives enough of a shit to lose it."

I sigh. "That's not true. I'm sure if you were in contact with your parents, they would lose their shit not hearing from you."

Luna frowns. "Doubt it."

Luna and her parents had a huge falling out when they caught here hacking at home. Not to mention, they were already pissed she was going to Brown to study computer engineering instead of following in the family's footsteps of becoming a lawyer. Her mom, her dad, and her sister are lawyers. But it's not what she wanted. Finding out she was hacking illegally for cash was the last straw and they lost their shit and kicked her out. So she hasn't spoken to them since.

It's sad, really. Luna is so successful. I don't get why her parents are so against computer engineering. After all, computers are the future.

"We've got to remain positive," I tell her. "If we let them break us before they even start, we're screwed."

Luna nods. "I know." Her eyes flash with fire. "I won't let them break me." Her voice lowers as she says, "But, Kali…" She trails off. "I'm not sure she can hold it together. I think they've already broken her."

I nod. "Out of all of us, Kali is the most fragile."

"Yeah, I don't know how she's going to handle it,"

Luna says, slumping back so she's lying on the haystack. It's scratchy and horrible to sleep on, and I miss the comfort of the hotel already. And the comfort of Taren's warm body against mine.

"He didn't touch you, did he?" Luna asks, breaking me out of my train of thought.

"What?"

"Taren? He didn't you know..." She looks uncomfortable.

"Rape me?" I ask.

She nods.

"No, he didn't."

"Thank God. I was worried he might have done something inappropriate. The way he looked at you that first day was..." She trails off, her brow furrowed. "Intense and possessive is the only way I can describe it."

"Yeah, it was a little weird," I admit.

But I don't share the full truth with them. That Taren did cross some boundaries. That there were inappropriate things he did, things which, against my better judgment, I found myself craving. It's a dangerous secret I keep, made even more menacing because I want it to happen again.

"I can't believe this is happening." Luna places a hand on her forehead. "We're going to die here."

I shake my head. "No, we're not."

"Since when are you the pinnacle of optimism?" Luna asks, as ordinarily I'm the skeptic. On this occasion, I've got a reason to be hopeful.

Taren promises to find a way to get me and my friends out. And for some crazy reason, I trust him. I trust a man I barely know. Maybe I'm the one that's mad and not him. Only time will tell if my trust is misplaced.

14

TAREN

The tension in the air is almost tangible. I lean against the stone pillar in the training room of the basement, watching Thiago circle the four prisoners like a predator. He lets his eyes linger on each girl for a few seconds. Whenever he looks at Alice, I feel a dark possessiveness claw at my throat.

Matias glares at me from the other side of the room. They're pissed that I'm here. After all, this is their territory. They're used to running this show, but I outrank them both.

Alice tries to make eye contact with me, but I've avoided looking at her as much as possible.

"You're now the property of the Navarro Cartel," Thiago announces.

The dark-haired girl from the other cell whimpers in response.

Matias looks like he feeds off her fear, baring his teeth. "Which means we'll train you to be good little sluts for your future owners."

Alice knows all of this because I told her in Mexico City. I notice how her bottom lip trembles and her already pale complexion pales further. I haven't got a plan. I rarely do. My motto is to act on instinct, as my instincts rarely steer me wrong.

Matias' leer shifts toward Alice again, and I see pure terror flashing in her eyes. That twisted part of me enjoys her fear. It's a sick thing to admit, but it's the truth. However, I want to be the one who controls her fear and every emotion here on in. Seeing Matias scares her only makes me more possessive. I must keep my jealousy in check, or they'll know something is up.

I walk forward, commanding the attention of the room. "Enough of the chit-chat. Let's get on with the training." I hope my interruption has veiled my concern for Alice, offering her a momentary respite from their predatory gazes.

My feelings must remain in darkness, buried under a ruthless facade, for her sake and mine.

Matias growls softly. "I don't know what you're doing here, Taren."

I tilt my head. "A change of pace."

Thiago rolls his eyes. "Fed up with warming Ileana's bed?"

Hot anger flashes through me.

A flash of jealousy and confusion enters Alice's sky-blue eyes. "Do you want me to cut your balls off?" I ask, walking forward and pulling my knife from my jacket pocket. "I'd happily show the girls what happens when you cross me."

Thiago is a proud fucking idiot, but he backs down. He knows I have no issue resorting to violence. It's my second language. He clears his throat. "Let's get on with it. Strip, girls," he demands.

The idea of these two fuckers seeing her naked makes my blood boil. However, there's no avoiding it.

Alice's eyes go wide at the request and she looks to me.

I clench my jaw and try to communicate through my eyes alone. I won't let them hurt her. But, then, seeing her naked is unavoidable.

One girl sobs.

Matias rolls his eyes. "There's always one."

Ignoring Thiago's comment, I turn to the trembling

girls, fighting back my guilt. "Look at me," I command, my voice sharp but not devoid of a twisted sense of compassion. They flinch at my tone but reluctantly raise their eyes toward me. "This isn't a request. It's a command. Do as we say, and it'll be easier for all of us."

The room fills with a tense silence. Alice's gaze doesn't waver from mine. I can see a glimmer of understanding. She knows I'm doing this to protect her, to keep her safe in this hellish situation.

"The first lesson is obedience," I continue, "Always remember that."

As the girls hesitantly undress, I keep a steady gaze on Alice, not out of desire, but to offer her an unspoken promise. I'll do whatever it takes to keep her safe, even if it means playing the villain for now.

The girls strip, but all of them stop at their underwear.

"Everything," I demand.

Alice grinds her teeth, and the other girls all look reluctant.

"Now!" I growl.

They flinch and strip off their underwear. All of them try to hide themselves from us with their arms over their chests. And when I look at Alice, she's glaring at me with betrayal in her eyes.

Oh, little bird. I thought you understood.

"Arms by your sides," Thiago barks.

All of them reluctantly put their arms down. My cock turns stiff at the sight of Alice's beautiful breasts and hard nipples. And the pure possessiveness that overwhelms me drives me insane when I see Thiago also admiring them.

Shit.

This is going to be difficult. It's not like I can murder my fellow soldiers for looking at her.

"All of you on your knees," I demand.

Thiago's jaw clenches. "This is my show, Hatter. Keep to the sidelines."

I glare at him and step forward. "I'm in charge."

Matias growls. "Like hell you are. This is our domain, so why don't you run along and be a good doggy for Illeana?"

I stalk toward him and grab him by the throat, squeezing hard.

His eyes widen, and he tries to claw my fingers away.

"What the fuck?" Thiago says, starting toward me.

I give him a glare. "I'm not a dog, and you two are beneath me," I spit. I release his throat, and he looks about ready to murder me.

I'd like to see him try. While Matias and Thiago are

two of Illeana's best fighters, they can't beat me. No one can.

The girls haven't moved an inch. "I said on your knees," I growl.

The four of them shakily drop to their knees, averting their gaze. The only one who keeps her head up is Alice, as she glares at me hatefully. Perhaps it's easier if she hates me for this. I can't free her, not yet.

I circle around them, ensuring I don't pay too much attention to my little bird, even though my blood is burning hot in my veins. Every part of my inner beast is clawing at my insides, wanting to take her from here and run far away where no one will ever find us. But I can't. Because there's nowhere I can go that Illeana won't find me.

"All four of you get on all fours like good little pets," I demand, playing the role expected of me.

Matias chuckles as he moves around so he's behind them. "Yeah, show us your pretty little cunts."

I grind my teeth. "Matias," I growl, glaring at him. "What did I say?"

His eyes narrow. "Fuck you, Taren. You can't just come in here and fucking censor us like some kind of tyrant." He rubs a hand across his cock. "We enjoy having fun with new prisoners."

Fucking bastard.

"Are any of you virgins?" I demand, ignoring him.

None of them put their hands up. That plan is out the window, then. A virgin slave has to remain intact because she'll fetch more money. It would have been a way to stop these rabid dogs from fucking them.

"Not the best crop, then. A virgin fetches four times the amount of money," I say.

Thiago snorts. "Have you got eyes? They're the four hottest pieces of ass we've ever had in here. We'll get a lot of cash for them."

Suddenly, the dark-haired girl who had been in the cell with Alice lifts her head. "If it's about cash, I can make you far more than what you'd sell me for."

Thiago growls and rushes over to her, grabbing her chin between his finger and thumb. "Don't speak unless spoken to, got it?"

Her eyes narrow, and she glares at him. The girl has fire.

The blonde one glances at Luna. "Don't do it," she breathes, barely audible.

"I'm one of the best hackers in North America, you sick son of a bitch. And I could make you guys a lot of money."

Thiago's eyes narrow a fraction. "We already have hackers."

Her eyes flash. "Your cartel does, right? But how about you personally?"

Clever girl.

Matias and Thiago are greedy fuckers. However, they won't want to agree to her deal in front of me because they think I'm loyal to Ileana. How wrong they are.

I see how Matias's and Thiago's eyes light up at the mention of money.

"Shut it, bitch," Thiago says, bringing his hand down across her face, but not very hard. I know if he wanted to hurt her, he would have struck her much harder than that.

While I'm not keen on Thiago or Matias, they could prove to be the perfect allies later down the road. All they care about is money. And I doubt they give a rat's ass about Ileana in reality, which means I could use them to my advantage. Get them on my side when the time is right.

I step forward and look at the four girls. "Imagine you're a puppet, pulling against your strings in a struggle for freedom. But the more you resist, the tighter the strings become. The puppeteer, the master of your fate, could snap the strings any moment. If you submit and dance to their tune, the strings loosen. You can move with ease and grace, creating an illusion of freedom. So, is the puppet truly enslaved, or does it hold the power by yielding to the puppeteer's touch?"

The same one who mentioned hacking looks at me. "You're fucking crazy."

I growl and grab her chin. "I'm not crazy. If you listen to what I'm saying, you'll realize the errors of your ways." I hit her then, knowing out of the four, she's clearly going to get the most shit because she can't keep her mouth shut. But I sense Matias likes that about her, which might be a blessing or a curse.

Alice has remained silent and still. Exactly like I coached her before we returned to the house.

Thiago steps forward. "So, puppet master, what's next in your grand performance?" There's heavy sarcasm lacing his words.

I don't bother looking at him.

I keep my gaze on the girls, particularly Alice. "Next," I say calmly, "we teach them how to dance." The sinister undertone in my words isn't lost, but I can tell Matias and Thiago are itching for a fight.

"Teach them?" Thiago scoffs, crossing his arms over his chest. "Since when did you become a dance instructor, Taren?"

I finally turn to them "I'm not talking about literal dancing, Thiago. It's a metaphor for control, for owning their destiny within the boundaries we set. Do you understand now, or should I use smaller words?"

Matias chuckles a low, dangerous sound that echoes in the room. He's enjoying the power play between the three of us.

Thiago uncrosses his arms.

"I'm saying," I continue, "that we need to mold them into obedient pets if we're going to get top dollar." I hate saying it because Alice is not a pet. She's my queen. My world.

Thiago clenches his jaw, a vein throbbing at his temple. "And what if they don't want to be molded, Taren?" His words are a cold, challenging whisper.

I feel a twitch of discomfort, but my gaze remains steady. "Then they'll learn what happens when they defy us. They're here to serve a purpose." My gaze lands on Alice again, and I soften my voice for her sake. "And they'll be rewarded for their cooperation. If not..." I let the threat hang in the air, knowing everyone in the room understands its weight.

Matias cracks his knuckles, an unnerving smile playing on his lips. "Then I suppose we better start 'teaching' them."

"How exactly do you propose we go about it?" Thiago asks.

"A task." I turn my attention back to the girls. "All

four of you on the bed," I demand, glancing at the bed in the training room.

They look horrified, but none of them refuse. All of them get up and sit on the edge of the bed.

"Lie down with your heads on the pillows next to each other," I demand.

They exchange nervous glances before doing as they're told. Their fear is keeping them obedient for now.

"And play with yourselves until you climax."

Matias and Thiago chuckle.

All four girls tense, looking at me with wide, horrified glances.

"You can't be serious?" The mouthy girl says.

As expected, she's the one that's going to get into the most trouble. "Do you want us to hurt you and show you how serious we are?" I ask.

Thiago steps forward. "I'll take and break her if you want, Hatter." He sounds a little too eager and I glance at him to see the fire in his eyes. He likes her. Perhaps because of the promise of hacking for him personally or because he wants her the way I want Alice.

Who knows?

"Fine," she says, moving her hand to her pussy and starting to pleasure herself.

The other girls follow suit. When I glance at Alice,

she's glaring at me with a hateful expression. Perhaps I didn't prepare her enough for what was to come. This beats what Thiago and Matias would be doing down here if I weren't taking the training. They probably would have raped all four of them by now.

The thought angers me. No one will go near Alice, or I'll chop their balls off and feed them to the dogs. Matias and Thiago had better be careful around her.

I glance over at the two men who both have their dicks in their hands. "Put your cocks away."

"Come on, man," Matias says, shaking his head. "You can't expect us to watch four hot as hell girls masturbating naked and not masturbate too. They need something to look at." Matias moves closer toward the quiet, timid one with dark brown hair who had been in the other cell. "Don't you, baby?" he asks, not touching her but getting close.

She doesn't look at him or his cock, shutting her eyes as she pleasures herself.

"You two are fucking vile," I announce.

"At least we're not fucking dead inside. Are you telling me your dick isn't hard watching them?" Thiago asks.

My cock is hard, but I'm not watching them. I'm watching one girl. Alice. And what I'd give to whisk her away from here and protect her from the depravity of my world. But it's not an option. Not yet.

For now, we have to lie in wait and bide our time. No matter how much it grates against the animal inside me, there's no other option. Every moment spent in this hellhole, watching her endure these indignities, it's like a thousand razor cuts to my soul. But patience is the only weapon I have in this twisted game.

And as much as it kills me to admit it, right now, this training is the only thing standing between Alice and the unforgiving brutality of the cartel's world. So I'll stay my hand, keep my secrets, swallow my rage for Alice. Because when the time comes, and it will, I'll make them all pay. Alice will be safe. And Ileana? She'll wish she never met met.

15

ALICE

I haven't felt this numb since the fated night two years ago with Professor Lovell. It feels like I gave Taren my trust, and he betrayed it, even though he made it clear he couldn't protect me. I'm not sure what I was expecting, but I think having him lead the sick and twisted games that unfolded a few hours ago made it worse.

Luna, Kali, and Blake have all been silent since. The sick thing is we all climaxed. Every single one of us. Shamefully played with ourselves in front of those men... No, they're not men. Beasts. And orgasmed for them under duress.

In fact, other than the orgasm Taren brought me to the night in the hotel, it was one of the most powerful I've felt. It's crazy the way the mind works. The twisted inner workings. We've all been put in the same cell this time rather than being split up.

Blake is the first one to break the silence, her voice barely audible, her words choked with shame. "I feel so dirty," she confesses, her gaze fixed on the cold stone floor.

Kali's hand finds hers, gripping it tightly in silent solidarity, her eyes never leaving the cell bars. Luna remains silent, staring blankly at the wall, lost in her own world of guilt and self-loathing.

"It's not our fault," I breathe.

Blake nods. "I know better than anyone. Our reaction was natural, but studying it versus actually experiencing it." She shakes her head. "And there's more shit to come. Worse."

Luna nods. "My big mouth is going to get me in trouble."

"We told you not to mention the hacking," Kali says quietly.

"I know." Luna shakes her head. "I just hoped it might have been a way out for us. I'm not going to lose hope," she announces, looking at us individually. "We need to stay positive like Alice said. What happened earlier was probably child's play. The only option is to be strong for each other."

The thud of approaching footsteps cuts off our

conversation. Taren appears before the bars, his eyes darker than the pitch-black night.

He looks straight at me, his gaze chilling and penetrative. And then he unlocks the cell door and advances inside. "Alice," he mutters my name. His cold, emotionless expression sends a shiver down my spine. "Come with me."

I rise to my feet, every fiber of my being screaming in protest.

He turns around and walks out of the cell, expecting me to follow.

I glance back at my friends, their eyes wide with fear, and then steel myself for the confrontation. It's time to face the beast.

I step toward him with a deep, shaky breath, reluctantly moving past the cell door.

He slams it shut and locks it. And then, he leads me further into the gloom, away from the comforting whispers of my friends.

I clench my fists, anger bubbling deep within. Taren didn't prepare me for the shit we had to endure today, and I sense it was only the beginning.

He pulls me close, the firm grip of his hand on my arm contrasting with the warmth I once felt. "Let me explain," he starts.

I pull my arm away, the spark of anger igniting into

flames. "What the hell was that, Taren?" I spit out. "You may not be able to save me from the training, but I didn't expect you to be the fucking psycho doling it out."

He bares his teeth. "You're angry? I saved you from certain rape by Thiago and Matias." He tilts his head. "And you're fucking angry?" He paces. "Little bird, they would have raped each of you at least once today. Hell, they'd do it regularly. But I'm a buffer." His dark eyes are full of dangerous rage as he looks at me. "I don't want them looking at you. I want to be the only man to ever see you naked again." He marches toward me and wraps his hand around my throat, squeezing. "But I've got no choice."

His words ignite a wild fury within me. "No choice?" I clench my fists. "You always have a choice." His grip tightens around my throat as his eyes burn into mine. "You could choose to let us go!"

A cruel smirk twists his lips. "Why would I do that, Alice?"

I swallow hard. "Why wouldn't you? You said you're going to save me and my friends."

"Yes. But I want you at the end of it, understood? I can't let you go because you belong to me."

I grind my teeth. "Then find me after, away from here," I suggest.

"If only it were that simple. Do you know how many security cameras Ileana has on the property?"

I shake my head.

"Six hundred and fifteen." He shrugs. "She's paranoid. And it's physically impossible for me to get you and your friends out of here without being seen on them. And that's not to mention the hundreds of guards patrolling the grounds and exits."

My shoulders slump.

"And so if I somehow managed to get you four out of here and safe. I would be giving myself a death sentence. Ileana wouldn't be lenient with me."

I sink my teeth into my bottom lip. "Why did that guy say you warm her bed?"

His expression hardens. "It's complicated."

"Is she your girlfriend?"

I scrunch my face up. "No, Ileana has brought me up since I was eight."

He told me he was eight when his house was burned down. "Since your house was destroyed?"

He nods.

"Did she do it?"

He doesn't answer; he merely stares at me blankly.

"Did she kill your family?" I ask.

His eyes shut, and his jaw clenches hard. "Yes."

"And she took you?"

He nods in response, nostrils flaring. "Yes."

It makes even less sense now. Why the fuck would a woman who raised him want her in his bed? That's sick.

"And she makes you sleep with her?" I confirm.

"Enough," he growls, squeezing harder. "I came to see you because I can't keep away. Because I can't have you thinking I'm the monster. I need you to understand. I need you to know I wouldn't do this if I had a choice."

I nod in response. "I understand," I breathe.

I've barely finished saying the word, and his lips descend over mine. Firm and warm as he kisses me desperately. It's a passionate kiss full of so much emotion. I taste the metallic tang of blood as his teeth press too hard into my lip, making me claw him closer. I deepen our kiss, wishing to spend the rest of my life in his arms.

I wrap my arms around his neck as he breaks the kiss. "I'm scared, Taren," I whisper.

He pulls back, his eyes hard as steel. "We're all scared, Alice," he retorts. "I'm doing everything I can to help you and your friends. But I need you to trust me."

Trust. It's not something I've been able to give easily since the night with Professor Lovell. I want to give it to Taren. I know deep down I do trust him. "Okay," I manage, trying to hide the tremble in my voice. "I trust you."

"Good," he says, a hint of relief in his voice. "Because it's going to get worse before it gets better. I need you to know that everything I do makes it more bearable for you."

"How long will we have to endure it?" I ask.

His jaw clenches, and he shakes his head. "I don't know, little bird. I need to select the opportune moment to strike."

"To strike Illeana Navarro?" I confirm, realizing his plan hinges on bringing down a powerful cartel leader.

"Yes. I'm close to putting my plan in motion."

"How can you stop someone as powerful as her?"

A flash of irritation enters his eyes. "What is always certain yet uncertain, never seen but always felt, a thin line between sanity and descent?"

I grind my teeth. "I'm not good at riddles." How can he be talking in riddles right now?

He grinds. "The future, little bird. I can't be certain I'll succeed in stopping the red queen, but it's already mapped out for us. For both our sakes, I hope I can stop her."

I sigh heavily. "Will you kill her?" I ask, wanting to understand what this man is capable of.

He nods. "Yes, there's no escaping the monster unless the heart stops beating. The Red Queen must bleed." He searches my eyes. "Does that scare you, little bird?" he asks, his voice barely above a whisper. "Does it frighten you that I'm willing to murder to keep you safe?" He grips my hips hard in a possessive hold. I'm entranced, caught in his gaze, the gravity of his words sinking in.

I shake my head. "No, because she deserves it for the terrible things she did to you."

He gazes into my eyes. "Before I met you, revenge was all that occupied my mind. And now you've taken its place."

This is crazy. He's crazy. We don't even know each other.

His lips descend on mine abruptly, violently. Our teeth clash, but neither of us cares. There's darkness in us; it feels like a wild storm when we come together. As if I'm the lighting to his thunder. His tongue delves into my mouth as though he's trying to drink me in.

"You're my everything," he growls into my mouth, his words muffled by the intensity of his kiss.

His everything.

I gasp for air, clutching his shirt in my fists. This is

madness. This man, this situation—it's all beyond comprehension.

Nothing has ever felt so right or real before. I slide my fingers into his hair, and he growls against my lips, circling my wrists with his hands and yanking them behind my back. He uses one hand to restrain them there, and the other caresses the bare flesh of my cleavage.

"I'm in control, little bird," he murmurs. His dark eyes appear almost black in the dim light of the basement.

"We shouldn't be doing this. What if—"

"I paid off the guard so no one will catch us." He kisses my neck. "And this is one of very few blind spots on her security cameras."

"Catch us doing what?" I breathe.

"This." He lifts me and perches me on some crates in the corner. And then he pushes me down so I'm on my back before pushing the hem of my dress up and groaning. "So wet for me, my little bird, aren't you?" He tilts his head, a dark madness flashing in his eyes. "I've missed your taste. One taste of you, and I was fucking addicted. I could spend the rest of my life devouring you and be happy."

I shudder, arching my back as his words stoke the

flames of desire. "Taren," I breathe his name. "This is crazy."

He raises a brow. "Is it? I think it's the most sane thing in the world." And then he devours me, his tongue lapping at my clit and sending lightning strikes of pleasure through me.

My body is on fire as his tongue delves into my pussy. The rough pad of his thumb circles my clit, making me pant for oxygen. Once I'm sure I'm on the edge, ready to shatter, he stops and gazes at me with dark eyes.

"Tell me how much you like it, baby. Tell me how much you like being at my mercy." He shoves a finger inside me, and I gasp, trembling for him.

"Answer me," he demands.

I nod. "I love it." My body thrums with desire as he chuckles.

"That's my good girl," he breathes, kissing my inner thigh and slowly moving closer to where I need to feel him. "Do you want more? Do you want me to devour you until you're screaming my name?"

I can hardly think past the desire which has taken control of my mind.

"Answer me." He spanks my inner thigh, and I gasp.

"Yes, I want more, please."

"Make me believe you, little bird." His wicked smile

sends a shiver down my spine. He leans in closer, tracing a path up my inner thigh with his lips until he's right there, so close to where I need him. "Beg me," he murmurs against my skin. The warmth of his breath sends sparks of pleasure coursing through me. "Beg me to taste you again."

His demand has my heart pounding in my chest, my mind a whirl of desire. "Taren," I whimper, my hips arching off the floor toward him. "Please," I groan, the words scraping raw from my throat. "Taren, lick me, taste me again."

His intake of breath is sharp, a hiss in the quiet room. He's waiting, I realize, for more. And I want to give it to him. I want to give him everything.

"I need you inside me," I whisper, desperation tinging my words. "Please, Taren, fuck me. I need you. I want you. Only you." The last words are a hoarse whisper, my voice breaking under the weight of my desire.

His dark eyes gleam with triumph and something darker, wilder. He grins, a predator ready to claim his prey, and I know, at this moment, I would give him anything he asks of me. "Sorry, little bird. But it's not time yet. I'll eat you, though, since you asked so nicely."

I grind my teeth, feeling irritated, and I'm about to

complain when he starts to finger me. And then he sucks my clit. His teeth gazing it softly.

My body convulses, a sharp gasp escaping me as his tongue works its magic. His hard gaze is locked on mine, watching, waiting for every reaction.

The world narrows down to this dark room, to him and me, the rough concrete crate beneath me, and the relentless pleasure he's drawing out of me with his mouth.

"Taren," I plead, my voice a raspy whisper.

He doesn't respond, licking me over and over. His thick fingers plunge in and out of my wetness. This time, when I feel myself near the edge, he doesn't stop. He drives harder, slamming his fingers into me with so much force I break apart.

My body convulses, pleasure ripping through me in waves, and my scream echoing around the room. When I return to earth, he's there, grinning at me wickedly, his lips glistening in the dim light.

"Good girl," he murmurs, his fingers gently tracing my inner thigh. I can only blink at him dazedly, my body still thrumming with aftershocks, my mind still reeling. "Now," he purrs, his fingers tracing lazy patterns on my skin, "it's time for you to go back into your cage, little bird."

His words break the spell. Reality comes rushing

back in, and I sit up, that ache returning in my chest. What if this is all a game to him? It's clear he's not exactly sane. And perhaps he likes to mess with girls they capture now and then. Tell them he'll break them free and act like he's protecting them when he's playing a game with them.

"Why are you looking at me like that?" he asks.

I shake my head. "Like what?"

"Like I shattered your heart into a million pieces."

"Perhaps because you did." I clench my fists. "You do every time you put me back in my cage."

He steps forward, cupping my face in his hands. "I never want to break your heart. It breaks mine putting you in there. But when the time is right, I'll destroy everyone that forced me into this position. I'll burn the world down until it's just the two of us."

"And my friends," I say.

He laughs. "And your friends."

I know my doubts are silly. Taren cares about me for some inexplicable reason, and I care about him. "Okay," I breathe.

He places a hand over my heart. "Be strong for me."

I nod in reply.

"Good girl," he replies, grabbing my wrist forcefully and dragging me back toward my cell. "I'll see you tomorrow," he breathes.

Then he unlocks the door and pushes me inside, locking it without glancing back.

I turn to face my friends. When I do, they're all looking at me with narrowed eyes.

"What the fuck was that?" Luna asks, hands on hips.

"What?" I ask.

Kali shakes her head. "There's no use lying, Alice. We heard you moaning his name."

A flood of heat travels through my body, making my cheeks burn. Shit.

"He was training me," I lie.

Luna steps forward. "Cut the shit. We're your best friends. If you've got the hots for the guy, just admit it. He's been into you since the day he set eyes on you."

I glance at Luna, then at Kali, and sigh heavily, dropping onto the hay-strewn floor. For a brief moment, I let the silence fill the room. "Alright," I begin, my voice barely a whisper. "You're right." I glance at my friends. "Sit down, and I'll tell you everything."

Taren insisted they couldn't know about his plan or our relationship, but it's too late. I'm a terrible liar, especially when lying to my three best friends.

16

TAREN

"On your knees," I demand, circling the four girls.

Thiago's jaw clenches as he steps forward. "They need more hands-on training, Taren," he growls.

Shit. It was only a matter of time until these guys lost their patience. It's been five days since their training started, and I've managed to hold the hungry wolves at bay. I know I can't much longer. I glare at him. "What do you suggest?"

"There's three of us and four of them. We can each be getting our dicks sucked at the very least," Matias suggests.

I snort, feeling a sudden rush of adrenaline at the suggestion. My cock throbs. The idea of shoving it down Alice's pretty little throat drives me wild. It's about time she got a taste of me. "You're mad, Matias," I snap.

Thiago growls. "Matias is right. They need to learn to obey while giving pleasure."

I grind my teeth. "Fine, I'll take Alice," I state, meeting her gaze.

She narrows her eyes but knows I don't have a choice. I tried. There's no way I'll let anyone else touch her.

"I'll take the pretty little hacker," Thiago says, smirking at Luna. "Come here, baby."

Luna is the most spirited of the four girls and glares at him. "I can't promise you won't lose it," she growls.

Matias laughs. "Careful, she might actually bite your dick off. The chick is crazy."

Luna glares at him. "Me, crazy? Have you looked in the mirror lately?"

Matias snaps then and stalks toward her, intent on inflicting pain, but I grab his wrist before he can get close. "Not right now." I glare at Luna. "Keep your mouth shut unless it's to suck cock. Got it?"

Luna looks into my eyes but finally relents, nodding. "Fine."

"I'll take Kali, the golden princess," Matias breathes, looking like a love-struck teenager as he stares at her.

The guy is obsessed with her, unfortunately for Kali. "And since that leaves the pretty, tall blonde, I'll take her too. Two mouths worshiping my cock." He unzips his pants and walks toward Kali, who glares at him."

Thiago walks to Luna and does the same. Leaving me standing there, feeling conflicted. The idea of fucking Alice's throat while she gags on my dick is undeniably enticing. The control, the dominance, the sheer thrill of it all. But at the same time, the thought of her being forced into this gnaws at me. I'm no saint. I've done things, bad things, but this...

"Are you going soft on us, Taren?" Matias taunts, his eyes wild.

"Never," I retort, my eyes locked with Alice's. She's mine. I made the choice. I'll bear the consequences. And I'll be damned if I let anyone else lay a hand on her. I walk over to her and unzip my pants. "Open your mouth."

Surprisingly, she doesn't look scared. The only thing flashing in her sky-blue eyes is desire as I pull my cock free. And then I remember her fantasy. My dirty little Alice likes this. Likes being held captive and told what to do. She likes being forced.

"Now," I growl.

She opens her mouth, and I slam the length of my cock to the back of her throat, making her gag. My thoughts whirl, a tempest of raw desire and gut-wrenching guilt. Alice is on her knees, eyes watering as she chokes on me. She likes this, wants this.

Every time she gags, I drive harder. The darkness within me takes over as tears gush down her face, and she stares at me with shock in her expression. I'm a monster, a deranged beast consumed by lust and power. And then I see her move a hand beneath her skirt as she plays with herself.

My dirty little bird.

She's getting pleasure from this. Pleasure from being used like a filthy slut. My gaze oscillates between her beautiful face, flushed with pleasure and the raw desire in her eyes, and her hands beneath her skirt, lost in the ecstasy of her own touch.

It's thrilling—seeing her like this, a willing partici-pant in this sick game. I feel a surge of possessiveness, a seething anger toward those witnessing this intensely private moment. But then again, I don't have a choice, do I?

Matias is grunting like a beast. "That's it, goddess. Choke on my cock!" He's slamming into Kali's mouth as if it were her cunt like a feral animal. Blake appears to be left out, kneeling nearby, keeping her eyes off the scene before her. It's clear Matias has a weakness for Kali.

Thiago, on the other hand, has Luna sitting on the hay as she sucks his dick. He's giving her more control, perhaps even more than I'm giving Alice. But then, Alice doesn't want control. She wants to be taken and used and fucked without mercy.

Right then, as Alice swallows around me, I catch a flicker of movement from the corner of my eye. Third wheel Blake, unable to look at the spectacle, is now being tugged by Matias. He's done with Kali, leaving her gasping for breath, a broken doll discarded on the rough hay.

He's all smiles, a smug satisfaction tugging at his lips as he maneuvers Blake, sinking into her throat.

The sick and twisted part of me enjoys this. Seeing these girls being used. And using my Alice at the same time. My cock swells. I grip her hair tighter, my groans echoing off the walls as I close my eyes and surrender to the overwhelming sensation of the debauchery of it all.

And yet, I know it'll only get harder to keep the wolves at bay now. They'll want to fuck all the girls, including Alice, and I can't allow that. A plan needs to be put in place as fast as fucking possible.

I can feel my climax building, a tide rising and swelling until it crashes. With a final, desperate thrust,

I spill my cum down Alice's throat. "Swallow," I growl, the command guttural and raw.

There's a moment of surprise in her eyes, a flicker of hesitation, but it's replaced quickly by a fierce, unwavering determination. Like the good girl she is, Alice swallows, taking every drop of me as her throat works around my pulsating length. "Good girl," I breathe.

Her eyes flash as she starts to shake, but she uses her free hand to clamp it over her mouth, knowing that it would be questionable if she came from sucking me off against her will. And I watch, committing the image to memory. I lean down and breathe into her ear. "You were such a good girl for me, weren't you? I can't wait to get you the fuck out of here so we can do that every fucking day."

She moans softly, but I swallow it with a kiss, tasting my own cum on her tongue.

The other two finally finish, pulling away from Luna and Blake with self-satisfied grins. The girls look up, their eyes shining with humiliation and despair.

Luna's eyes are downcast, avoiding all contact, while Blake's gaze is blank, detached from reality. Lips swollen, cheeks flushed with shame, their pretty faces are a stark reminder of the debased circus we've made of their lives.

Thiago turns to me. "How about their cunts now? Their mouths aren't enough."

Matias grins. "Yeah, let's fuck them until they're begging us for more like dirty little whores."

"No," I growl, glaring at them both. "That's enough. I told you these girls must remain as pure as possible for their buyers. No one wants sloppy seconds."

Matias and Thiago look irritated by that. "You're a fucking killjoy."

"Perhaps this is why we haven't been getting top dollar for the girls recently because you aren't going about their training right." I set my hands on my hips. "I'm putting an end to that."

Alice shoots me a look, something akin to gratitude in her eyes. Despite the darkness within me, I can't help but be affected by it. I turn away, refusing to let the others see any hint of weakness.

"Come on, let's leave the girls to rest," I command, my voice steady.

Thiago and Matias file out of the room.

As the cell door closes behind them, I turn to Alice, Luna, Blake, and Kali. Their once vibrant eyes now hold a glimmer of desolation, a stark contrast to the fiery spirits they once possessed.

"Get some rest," I bark, clipping my tone because Thiago and Matias will hear me. However, I keep my gaze steady on Alice, trying to communicate through my eyes how sorry I am that it came to this.

She holds her chin high and gives me a slight nod. "Yes, sir," she breathes.

The three other girls look completely broken as they sit huddled on the hay bales, but not my Alice. My little bird is a fighter. And she'll need to be strong to survive this game we're playing.

17

TAREN

That evening after we violated the girls, Ileana asks me to dinner.

We rarely eat together, but she said we're expecting a guest. It can't be Damien Vasquez, as he clarified that he wouldn't be attending any meeting Ileana proposes. I don't blame him. She's a fucking psychopath.

I glance at my reflection and adjust my tie, ensuring it's perfect before stepping out. I know damn well appearances matter in this godforsaken business. And if Ileana has guests, I must look my best. Even if I'm wearing a pair of emerald suit pants and a grey jacket, which will piss her off.

I walk downstairs and toward the dining room, where soft voices echo. Whoever this 'guest' is, they're already here, and by the tone of the voice, the guest is male. When I get to the doorway, I freeze in my tracks. Gaston Marques. Why the fuck is that sick bastard here?

He's not here for the world-class steak tartare or the aged scotch. No, he can only be here for one thing. For the girls. My gut clenches, Alice. I swear if he so much as thinks about her, I'll bathe in his blood. I don't care how rich he is. Ileana knows they aren't ready.

But I've got to be smart about this. I can't let my temper get the best of me, not when there's so much at stake. I put on a plastic smile, the one I've perfected over the years, and stride into the room. "Gaston, what a surprise," I say.

Ileana flashes me a warning glance as I take my seat, but I ignore it. "I told you we were having a guest," she says.

I glare at her. "You didn't say who, though, did you?" I tilt my head. "You realize they've hardly started their training."

Gaston claps his hands. "Perfect. You know I prefer a hands-on approach with my girls."

I can't stop the shudder that runs down my spine at those words. The fucking pervert. But I have to be careful. He's a customer and a high-paying one at that.

I grit my teeth and force a nod. "Of course, Gaston. Whatever you say."

I glance at Ileana, who looks satisfied. That woman is a snake.

"Are we eating first, or do you wish to see the girls?" I ask, keeping my voice steady.

Gaston smirks. "I'd love to see the girls first."

I nod and lead him out of the room and down the hallway toward the door to the basement, ignoring the sick feeling in my gut. If he even thinks about selecting Alice... I don't know what I'll do. Carnage will ensue, and it'll be terribly bloody.

When we reach the cell, I clear my throat.

"On your feet, girls. You've got a visitor."

The four girls stand to their feet as instructed, with their arms behind their backs and eyes on the floor.

"Not completely untrained, are they, Taren?"

I don't look at him. "They've been training for a few days."

I unlock the cell door and walk inside, trying not to focus too much on Alice. It's hard. She consumes me. Anytime I'm near her, I crave her.

Gaston begins to inspect the four girls, circling them. Each time he nears Alice, I feel my muscles tense, ready to spring into action. It's like a vile game of Russian roulette, and I'm forced to watch with her fate out of my hands.

"Why don't you tell me about this one?" Gaston points at Alice.

I feel a surging tide of rage threatening to burst forth. The beast speaks of my Alice like she's an object on a shelf. Not like the queen she is.

"That's Alice," I say. I can barely look at her, fearing what my face might betray. "She's spirited." My attempts to sound detached are failing miserably. I can hear the trembling undertone in my voice, the barely restrained fury. All it would take is one wrong move, one indication that he intends to choose Alice, and I would snap. The consequences be damned.

Gaston chuckles a sound that grates on my nerves like sandpaper. "Spirited, eh? I do enjoy a good challenge." He moves closer to Alice, reaching out to lift her chin.

I ball my hands into tight fists, the knuckles white.

"But the spirit can be broken, can't it, Taren?" His eyes meet mine, a smirk playing on his lips. He knows. How, I couldn't say. He's baiting me. I know he is. It takes all of my willpower not to rise to it. Not to reach out and snap his neck right here and now. He drops his hand and turns to Kali. Matias' obsession.

The fury still boils beneath my skin, the need to

protect Alice and shield her from this world. But I can't. Not yet. Not without risking everything.

Gaston checks over each girl, but his attention remains on Blake the longest. "And who's this?" He asks, his interest piqued.

"Blake," I answer, my voice flat. He doesn't need to know more. He simply needs to move on from Alice.

"Blake," He says, his hand moving to her chin as he lifts it and searches her eyes. "She's the one. I'll take her."

Kali gasps beside her. "No!" She breaks all protocol and falls out of line. "You can't take her! You sick son of a bitch."

I walk over to Kali and slam my hand into her face, forcing her to the floor. "Apologies for that, Gaston. We'll sort out the paperwork over dinner. I'll have Pedro prepare her for you."

A dark side glance catches my attention as Gaston's laughter fills the room. It's Alice. Her eyes, normally so vibrant, hold a biting glare as sharp as a dagger. Her gaze is locked on me, full of accusations I can't deny.

Her hands form into tiny fists at her sides, shaking with suppressed fury. Blake is her friend. And I'm selling her friend to a beast. I've got no choice.

In this wicked game, choice a luxury I can't afford. There's no room for sentimentality or morality in a world that thrives on exploitation. I told Alice I'd get her friends out. Perhaps that was a mistake on my part. I'm a player bound by invisible chains, condemned to make unthinkable decisions.

I condemn Blake to a life she didn't choose, just as I was condemned. It's a cycle of despair. I'll break the cycle soon, and once I do, we can rescue her friend, but we've got to play along for now.

Her gaze is a silent scream of betrayal that drowns out everything else. I look away, the weight of her stare too much.

"Perfect," Gaston says. "I look forward to playing with you, my pretty little vixen."

Blake looks up at him right in the eyes. "Fuck you," she spits.

The smirk on Gaston's face widens. "I'm going to have fun with this one, Taren. Aren't I?"

I nod. "It would seem so."

Without another word, I turn on my heel, leading Gaston away from the holding cells. The lock clangs behind us, echoing through the corridor like a death knell.

We return to the dining hall, the air thick with anticipation. Ileana is waiting, a false cheerfulness plastered on her face. Her gaze flits toward us, and she rises from her seat. Her movements are always so calculated and smooth. "Gaston, Taren," she greets us with a smile that doesn't reach her eyes. "How did you find our girls?" she asks, looking at Gaston.

Gaston runs a hand through his chestnut brown hair. "Beautiful. I selected one of them." He tilts his head. "Usual price?"

Ileana clears her throat. "These are more expensive, as I explained on the phone." She pulls out a seat at the table. "Come, sit, and eat, and we'll discuss the details."

Gaston nods, easing himself into the chair, his gaze fixed on Ileana. "We can negotiate," he says, his tone dismissive.

Alice is angry because I couldn't protect Blake. When will she realize how little power I've got over operations here?

Ileana sits at the head of the table, smirking. Every fiber of my being hates the woman before me.

Gaston is a pig. The kind of man I wouldn't want to call my friend. However, it's not him that I hate. Normally, we get on okay. He's intelligent and quick-witted and often can decipher my riddles. I guess he'd have to be smart to own a billion-dollar software company he built from the ground up. The headquarters are in Mexico City, where Blake will end up.

"I want fifteen million and not a penny less," Ileana says as she sips on her glass of wine. "Agreed?"

He chuckles. "That's five million more than your standard fee."

Her jaw clenches. "I've seen the girls. All four of them are worth five million more because none of them are *standard*. They're more beautiful than any girls you've purchased from me before. Fifteen million, or I'll sell them to the highest bidder." Her eyes narrow. "I'll get over fifteen, I'd expect, for the one you want. Blonde, right?"

Gaston leans back, still smirking, but his eyes have a dangerous spark. "Yes, and tall."

Ileana nods. "She's supermodel standard. Perhaps if you don't want to pay—"

"Fifteen it is," he says simply. "Get your man to write up the contract."

I glare at Gaston, my eyes searing into him. "I'm not a fucking lawyer," I reply.

He knows that, but he always tries to wind me up. Ever since he learned how strained the relationship is between Ileana and me the first time he visited, it's been the same.

Ileana clears her throat, trying to ease the tension. "My lawyer will be here shortly to sort it out."

Gaston nods and leans forward, helping himself to

the food on the table. "Perfect." He leans back and takes a sip of his wine. "Now that business is out of the way, how have you been, Ileana?"

I clench my fists beneath the table, waiting for her response.

"Not the best." Her eyes narrow. "Have you heard about the Estrada cartel trying to secure Mexico City?"

Gaston sits up, tension coiling through his muscles. "No," he says, but I sense it's a lie from the tone of his voice. He knows about it.

"Don't lie to me, Gaston." Ileana knows it's a lie, too.

Gaston is influential in Mexico City. He's one of the richest men in Mexico, if not the richest. "I may have heard some rumors, but nothing more."

"Tell me everything you've heard," Ileana demands.

He sips his scotch. "Just that he's making waves and buying up real estate in the city."

I didn't want Gaston to confirm anything, but this information will further cement the idea in Ileana's mind.

"So, he's trying to gain control?" Ileana murmurs, pulling out her phone and typing something furiously.

Gaston watches her. "I wouldn't worry too much,

Ileana. No one has controlled Mexico City for centuries." He shakes his head. "I doubt Pablo Estrada will change that."

He just might. I've got a meeting with him in a few days. It's a risk, allowing him to see my face, but one I must take. If I remove Ileana from her throne, I need powerful backing. As the Navarro Cartel will be easy pickings. I'll be the one to take it, but I expect a fight on my hands.

I may be the only one with the Navarro name since Ileana gave it to me when I was eight, but I'm not a Navarro, not by blood. And blood is what speaks around here. Ileana has no blood relatives left. She either killed them, or they died of old age.

Time is of the essence, especially since Ileana is being unpredictable. Asking Gaston here a few days into the girl's training makes no sense. And yet here we are, agreeing a deal for one of Alice's friends. If Gaston had wanted Alice, I know that I would have burned the entire place to the ground to get her out and probably would have died in the process.

She's a dangerous distraction that I didn't need. And I can only hope she won't be my undoing rather than my salvation.

18

ALICE

"What are we going to do?" Blake asks, pacing the floor. "That fucking bastard is going to buy me!"

I'm so angry at Taren. He said he'd get all of us out before his boss tried to sell us. Yet here we are with Blake about to be sold to a ridiculously handsome yet cold and creepy man. God knows what his story is. Or what he'll do to her.

All I know is Blake will face a life of slavery if we don't stop this. And the look Taren gave me suggests he can't stop it. It's out of his hands.

"Let's try the vent again," Luna suggests, staring up at the air vent, which they secured tighter since I tried to climb out of it.

I shake my head. "We've got no chance of getting

out of there. It was too tight once I actually stuck my head in. We'd probably all get stuck."

Kali paces back and forth. Out of the three of us, she's been struggling the most with this entire situation from the start. And the longer we're here, the deeper her cracks are getting. She spins around. "We can't just let him take her. We have to fight this!"

I clench my jaw. "If we fight, all four of us will end up dead or worse. Fighting these people will only make our situation unbearable."

Kali shakes her head. "So, what's the option? Let that guy take her?"

Luna walks up to Kali and grabs her hand, squeezing. "This is about survival now." She glances at Blake. "And Blake is strong."

Blake nods. "I'll try my best to escape and rescue you guys."

"We make a pact right now. Whoever gets out first comes to rescue the others, okay?" Luna suggests.

We all nod and place our hands in a circle together.

A palpable sense of determination ripples through the room as our hands stack together. A fire blazes in their eyes, matching the heat of the pact we've just made. "We're in this together, to the bitter end," Kali says through clenched teeth. "We survive, we escape, we come back for the others. Remember, we're stronger than they think we are."

I'm glad to see she's back to her fighting self. The initial shock of our situation broke her spirit, but not for long. She's tougher than that.

The room falls eerily silent after her declaration. We know the road ahead won't be easy, but we stand a chance together. The bond we've formed in this wretched place is our greatest weapon. And with a resilience born out of desperation, we steel ourselves for future battles.

It feels like we're waiting in silence for an age until we hear the telltale signs of a door creaking in the distance, followed by footsteps. After a while, Matias, the crazy one, appears, smirking at us.

"Looks like Gaston has a liking for blondes. Blake has been purchased, so I'm going to get her ready."

Matias strides forward, his cold, predatory gaze locked on Blake. The room fills with a palpable tension that feels like a physical force.

I can't stand here and do nothing. "Not so fast, creep!" I lunge at Matias, which is stupid, but I'm running on adrenaline.

Matias doesn't blink an eye as he gives me a swift backhand, sending me sprawling across the floor. I groan in pain as I fall funny, and my face stings. The impact will leave a bruise.

"Don't try anything else," he warns.

Kali follows suit and punches him in the stomach when he's distracted, and then Luna kicks him in the shin. Both of them are crazy. But Matias merely growls at Luna and doesn't raise a hand to her before turning and grabbing Kali, pushing her against the wall. Horror floods me as I realize his intention. He yanks her dress up to her hips, revealing her torn panties.

He whispers something into her ear. I see her body stiffen, the color draining from her face.

Suddenly, there's a change in the atmosphere, a shift so profound that it's almost tangible. I can't process what's happening. It's like time slows down, and for a moment, everything is silent. Then it hits me. Rage, pure, unadulterated rage. My blood is boiling with a fury I didn't know I had. "Get off her, you sick bastard!" I scream, throwing myself at Matias with renewed energy.

He simply laughs, a grotesque sound echoing in the room. But he doesn't move away from Kali. This isn't just about power for him. It's about control. Control over us. This is a game, and we're his playthings.

What I can't work out is why Luna got off so easily.

But perhaps that's because Matias' brother, Thiago, has a weakness for her. They're both sick in the head. Suddenly, I hear someone clearing their throat behind me and turn to see Taren standing there.

"What the fuck do you think you're doing, Matias?"

Matias, looking startled, turns his head to face Taren. His eyes narrow and the smirk drops as he releases Kali. She slumps against the wall, gasping for breath.

An eerie silence settles in the room; you could cut the tension with a knife. "I was asked to retrieve the girl, Taren," Matias growls, his eyes glinting dangerously. "Which means I'll do it however I see fit. It's none of your business."

Taren steps forward, his face a mask of controlled rage. "It became my business when you laid your hands on them," he retorts in an icy cold voice.

The man who wants to buy Blake steps into the cell. "And I don't like how you treat the assets I'm paying for."

Matias growls. "You're only buying one, and I didn't touch her."

The man stands tall, striding toward Matias. "Maybe not on this occasion, but if you treat the girls this way once. You'll do it all the time." He runs a hand through his dark brown hair. "Perhaps I'll cancel my sale and tell Ileana I don't like how her men treat the assets I'm paying top dollar for."

Matias backs off, eyes narrowing. "I apologize. It won't happen again."

The man walks toward Matias, his pale blue eyes assessing him. There's a lethal edge to the man dressed in a sharp suit with no hair out of place. I dread to think of what he'll do with Blake once he gets her alone. A shiver races down my spine. Once he's directly in front of Matias, he grabs him by the throat. "Perhaps I should murder you right here and now. I'm not a fool. You've put your hands on my asset more than once since she arrived here, haven't you?"

Matias struggles to draw in air, his dark eyes bulging as he grabs the man's wrists.

Taren clears his throat. "Gaston, please release my man." His voice is calm, but I see a hint of concern in his eyes.

Gaston, the man who is buying Blake, must be dangerous.

Gaston releases Matias, stepping back with an icy smile. "Your man needs to learn his place, Taren." He says, fixing his cufflinks with a nonchalant air. "As for the asset..." His gaze slides to Blake. She stands as rigid as a statue, fear etched into her features. "I trust she'll be worth every penny." With that, he exits the cell.

A tear slides down Blake's cheek, but she quickly brushes it away. I hate this. I hate how powerless we are. I glare at Taren, who's still standing there staring at me. Matias is clutching his throat.

"That son of a bitch almost killed me," he growls, standing to his feet with his fists clenched.

"About time someone taught you a lesson," Taren replies, eyes still fixed on me. "Did you strike Alice?" he asks, his voice has a lethal edge.

I bring my finger to the spot where Matias back-handed me and wince. There's obviously a bruise which made Taren aware of his treatment of me.

Matias growls at him. "What the fuck is with your obsession with Alice?"

Taren doesn't even blink at the question. He's as cool as a cucumber as he stares at Matias. "Did you strike her?" he repeats the question.

Matias folds his arms over his chest. "She fucking came at me. So, I stopped her."

It's true. I did try to attack the bastard, so it's not like he struck me for no reason. But Taren's rage feels like a tangible entity between us, simmering like lava beneath a volcano ready to erupt.

Before I can react, Taren lunges at Matias, knocking him to the ground with one swift, powerful punch. His fists are a blur as they connect with

Matias's face repeatedly. "You don't touch her," he hisses through gritted teeth, punctuating each word with a punch. The air crackles with raw, primal fury. I've never seen this side of Taren before. It's terrifying, and yet, there's a part of me that's relieved. Relieved that someone is finally standing up for us, for me.

Matias puts up a fight, but Taren's power and strength are unmatchable. Every time Matias lands a punch, Taren shows no sign of pain. He doesn't react.

Blood spatters on the grimy floor beneath them. It's a gruesome sight, yet none of us move to intervene. Eventually, Taren pulls back, panting heavily. His knuckles are raw and bleeding, but he doesn't notice.

His icy gaze meets mine, a silent promise that he won't let Matias touch me again. Matias groans on the floor, a bloody, beaten mess. I don't feel a shred of sympathy for him.

The tension in the room is palpable. Taren's outburst has left us all shaken. A cruel reminder of the violence that lurks beneath the surface of our captors. Worst of all, Blake is going to be sold.

The room spins as the reality of our situation sinks in. Blake is going to be taken away, and nothing can stop it. We're going to be separated. The thought is like a punch to the gut, intensifying the pain that's already there.

Her absence will leave a gaping hole in our little group, a painful reminder of the friend we've lost and the dire situation we're stuck in. I don't want to imagine a day without Blake's humor to lighten the mood, without her strength to lean on. But I have to.

Because in this hellhole, reality bites, and it bites hard. It's a brutal awakening from the bubble we've been living in, assuming somehow we'd make it out of here alive and together. A bubble that's now burst leaving us cold and scared.

We'll fight. We'll survive. But for now, we're just four broken souls held captive in a nightmare, praying for dawn.

19

TAREN

I stop outside of the Red Queen's office, grinding my teeth. She rarely summons me to her office, which means she's angry. My meeting with Estrada is meant to be tomorrow, and I fear she might know somehow. If I get any sense she knows, I'll have to cancel. And Estrada isn't a patient man.

I knock and wait for her reply.

"Come in."

I open the door, narrowing my eyes when I see her splayed out on the couch, eating grapes. "You asked for me?"

"Indeed, Taren." Her voice is as cold as the frost outside. She tosses a grape into her mouth, watching me with a predator's interest. "I hear you've been meddling with the girls' training. Matias and Thiago aren't pleased."

I cross my arms, holding her gaze, "They're not doing it right. Gaston—"

She raises a slim finger, cutting me off. "Your job isn't to question their methods. You'll step back or bear the consequences."

I shake my head. "We almost lost Gaston's sale when he witnessed what Matias was doing with the girls," I protest, unwilling to let this go that easily.

Her eyes narrow. "I'll confirm that with Gaston directly, but until then, I've got another job for you."

"Go and meet with Damien Vasquez today," she commands, her voice dripping with authority. I clench my fists, seething beneath the surface.

"He refused a meeting," I reply, knowing that having to go to see Damien will make my meeting with Pablo impossible.

She continues to pop grapes into her mouth. "With me, but not with you."

"You're going to send me into the lion's den?" It's a dangerous meeting, but she doesn't care. She never does. All that matters to her is power and control.

Her eyes narrow as she glares at me. "You're becoming rather disobedient lately."

I can feel the tension between us crackle, a tangible

force ready to explode. I'm skating on thin ice and too close to the edge of destruction. If I'm too brazen and too reckless, she could sense my intent.

I take a deep breath, tamping down the anger that threatens to spill out. "Alright," I say, my voice controlled. "I'll meet with Vasquez." I take one last look at her, the Red Queen, in all her icy splendor, before turning on my heel and exiting the room.

Once outside, I lean against the wall, letting out a sigh. I need to speed up my plan. As much as it kills me to admit, Ileana's right. I've become disobedient and too obvious. But Alice needs someone to protect her. Matias and Thiago are two men ruled by nothing but their primal urges. If I don't do something now, it'll be too late.

A grim smile tugs at my lips. Time to put my plan into motion. Time to play the game by my rules.

I take a moment to settle my nerves, to rein in the storm raging within me. Then, I push off the wall and go to the basement. The corridor appears longer than usual, echoing with the thud of my footsteps.

When I get to Alice's cell, I hesitate. And then I appear before the bars, gazing at the three girls. This is the first time I've been to her alone since her friend, Blake, was taken by Gaston two days ago.

Her eyes narrow when she sees me.

I unlock the cell door. "Alice, I need to speak with you."

"Then you can do it in front of my friends," she replies coldly.

Doesn't she realize I had no power over Gaston taking her friend? It was out of my hands.

"Now," I growl.

My tone startles her, making her stand. She walks out of the cell, leaving her friends behind.

Once Alice is out, I lock it and lead her out of earshot of the other girls.

"You bastard," she says, her voice shaking. "You said you'd get us all out. The four of us!" She hits me then, and I grab her wrist, stopping her.

"I didn't have a choice," I snarl, wrapping a hand around Alice's throat and slamming her against the wall. My anger boils over, an uncontrollable tempest, and I let it flare despite my love for her. "You think I wanted this?" I spit out, my words harsh. "You think I wanted to see Blake taken away? You think I want you here, at her mercy?"

Her eyes flash with terror and regret sears through me, but the fury keeps spilling out. I'm no longer in control.

"I'm doing everything I can!" I hiss, my grip on her neck tightening. "And it's tearing me apart."

Her lip wobbles, and a few tears escape her eyes. "I know," she breathes.

Her statement eases my rage. Drawing a shaky breath, I release my grip on her neck. "Listen carefully, little bird," I tell her, forcing my voice to remain steady. "I'm putting my plan in motion. I'll unseat Ileana from her throne, but it won't be easy. It's far more complex than you can imagine." I pause, looking into her eyes, pleading with her to understand. "But you need to trust me. I've got to protect you from Matias and Thiago now more than ever. Ileana has ordered me to leave them to train you."

The fear in Alice's eyes cuts me like a knife. "But, they'll…" She trails off, unable to say it. They'll rape her and her friends if I don't find a way to stop them. Thiago's the only one I can try to reason with out of the two. Matias is a psycho. He doesn't listen to anyone but his brother, so I need Thiago on my side.

"I won't let them. I promise. I'll die before another man touches you," I growl. The possession over her I feel is fierce, primal. It's an emotion so deep it startles me. "I'll kill them first," I add, my voice barely a whisper now. "I'll kill them and fucking bathe in their blood. And then we'll lose ourselves to our passion while they lie on the ground lifeless."

My depraved fantasy makes Alice gasp, but when I look into her eyes, all I see is desire.

"Does that excite you, little bird?"

"Yes," Alice answers, her voice trembling. "Yes, it does." The admission shocks us both, but this is why I'm so drawn to her. She's perfect for me.

"Good, you must trust me," I respond.

She nods. "I trust you." She rises on her tiptoes, pressing her lips against mine.

Tension and desire slam into me as I freeze for a moment before grabbing her hips and deepening the kiss. My tongue thrusts into her mouth as my hands roam every dip and curve of her body.

This is reckless. Any of the guards could walk down here and see us. But I can't find it in me to care. My fingers tease the hem of her dress. She gasps into the kiss as I push her against the wall, lifting her against it.

I slip my hand under her dress, lifting her thigh and making her tremble.

She arches her back, inviting me to keep going.

Her cunt is so damn wet as I run my fingers through her. She moans into my mouth as I thrust two fingers inside. I keep my eyes locked on hers as I finger her roughly. Her legs wrap around me as I press her weight against the wall, trapping her between my body and the rough stone.

"Taren," she murmurs my name. "Please."

I know she's begging for more. She wants me inside her, but it's not time. "Not yet, little bird."

She grunts in frustration, eyes flashing with a fiery irritation. "When?" she demands.

I chuckle against her skin. "So eager. Soon."

She grunts as I finger her harder and faster, the wet sound of my fingers moving in and out mingling with her moans, creating a dirty symphony of pleasure. It's the most perfect sound I've ever heard. Her pleasure heightens, and the evidence is felt in the way her muscles grip me.

"That's it, baby," I groan, feeling the tightness around my fingers. Alice is on the edge of the precipice of pleasure. "Be a good girl for me. Come on my fingers."

Her body responds immediately, her inner walls clenching around my fingers. A primal moan escapes her lips. The sound of her pleasure is an intoxicating and sweet melody that I can't get enough of.

Her fingers dig into my arms as she cries out. I press my lips to hers to swallow her cries of pleasure.

I keep fingering her through her climax, the feel of her tightening around my fingers enough to drive me wild. What I'd give to have her come on my cock, but as I told her, it's not time.

As she comes down from her high, her body limp against the wall, I pull my slick fingers from her. I lift them to my mouth and suck them clean. "That's my good, delicious girl," I say, my voice rough with desire.

The following silence is laden with tension, a palpable energy that singes the air. "What now, Taren?" Alice asks.

I smirk, running a hand through my disheveled hair. "Now," I say, "we dance with the shadows and devour the silence, little bird."

Her brow furrows. "Why've you got to be so cryptic all the time?"

I tilt my head. "Would you prefer I be boring?"

She presses her lips together. "No, I just can't work you out half the time."

Ignoring her confusion, I reach out to gently touch her cheek. "We need to get you back to your cell," I say, my voice suddenly serious. "But don't worry, I'll figure out a plan."

Alice's lip trembles slightly. "I hope you do," she breathes.

I guide her back to the cell. The iron bars starkly contrast the heat of the moment we shared. As I secure the lock, I resist the urge to look back and meet her hopeful eyes.

There's no room for sentimentality. Not when there's a war to wage against a queen. I leave without a backward glance, letting the chilling silence of the cell echo behind me. Now, it's time. Time to set in motion a plan that's been brewing in the shadows of my mind for years. The moment has come to stir the waters, to light the fuse. The storm is about to begin.

20

TAREN

*T*hiago opens the door to his quarters, his eyes narrowing when he sees me standing there.

"What the fuck do you want?" he spits.

I hold my hands up in surrender. "I merely want to talk."

His eyes narrow further. "Talk about what? I'm not telling Ileana to let you back on. You're fucking up everything."

I grind my teeth, realizing the fact I beat up his brother yesterday won't go in my favor. Getting him on my side will be even more difficult .

"It's not about that. I think you'll want to hear what I have to say."

Thiago unwillingly opens the door. "Fine. Come in."

I enter his room, which is bare and basic. After all, most of the men live in squalor compared to me. Ileana's toy gets the best things, I guess.

I take a cursory glance around the room, taking in the shoddy state of his lodgings. The floorboards creak under the weight of my boots, their groans echoing through the room's hollow, almost skeletal structure. Unadorned walls, tainted by age and neglect, stand on either side, sparsely decorated with a few relics.

A single window, cloudy with grime and barely letting in any light, gives a grim view of the life outside. A lone bed lies in the corner, its sheet thread-bare and mattress sagging. It starkly contrasts my luxurious quarters, reminding me of the class divide that riddles our organization. The divides I intend to use to my advantage to throw Ileana off her throne.

"So, what do you want to talk about?" Thiago asks.

I lean against the door frame, my heart pounding with the weight of what I'm about to propose. "You ever thought about how things would be without Ileana calling the shots?"

Thiago snorts, crossing his arms over his chest. "And who's going to take her place? You?"

I glare at him. "Yes, and you and Matias."

Thiago's eyes narrow. "What?"

"We could run the cartel far better than she has. Share the ridiculous wealth she hoards." I glance around the room. "It sure looks like you could do with a share."

He growls. "This is all she gives most of the men. Hell, my rooms are better than a lot of the soldiers. Most of them live in fucking barracks on bunk beds."

"Then, let's change everything."

Thiago's eyes flicker with interest as he leans back against the dresser in the corner. "Killing Ileana and taking over the Navarro Cartel? What makes you think we can pull that off?"

I straighten, a cynical snort escaping my lips. "I've known Ileana longer than any of you," I start. "I know her strengths, but more importantly, her weaknesses. She's grown complacent and arrogant. She thinks she's untouchable, and that'll be her downfall."

"She's dangerous, Taren," Thiago says, a flicker of fear in his eyes. "How do you propose we do this?"

Pathetic.

I hate how all the men fear her. She's a woman. Flesh and blood. She can bleed just like any of us. And she's not exactly loved amongst the men. Fear might keep people in line, but it's not as valuable as respect. And to earn respect, you've got to give it.

"We give the men respect," I say, watching the man I've chosen as my second on this. "We treat them like humans, not mere pawns in Ileana's game. You think these men wouldn't turn on her if given a chance?" I pause, glancing at Thiago. "Wouldn't you?"

Thiago is silent, mulling over my words. "You're talking about a revolution, but revolutions are bloody and dangerous."

"And so is staying in this hell," I retort, gesturing at the shabby room. "Living under her thumb, waiting for the day she decides you're no longer useful. Is that the life you want for you and Matias?"

He frowns, deep in thought. And then, he nods slowly. "You're right," he says, a newfound resolve in his voice. "It's time for a change. And if it means getting my hands dirty, so be it." He tilts his head. "Why now?"

A good question that I'm unsure I should answer. However, honesty is going to be important if we're going to do this together. "Alice."

His eyebrow raises. "What?"

"I'd planned to do this for year, but her arrival here has forced my hand. She's mine."

Thiago's lips curve as he smirks. "I thought you

were hooked on her. Matias didn't believe me." He sighs heavily. "I'm a little bit obsessed with the beautiful hacker, honestly."

"Luna?"

He nods. "She'll be mine if we pull this off, got it?"

I clench my jaw, as that won't sit well with Alice. Unless Luna wants Thiago, it'll be a very tough sell. "What if Luna isn't interested."

His smirk widens. "Believe me, she's interested."

This piques my interest, as Luna hasn't shown any clear indication that she's interested in Thiago, at least not that I've seen. "Okay, but you can't take her against her will, agreed?"

"Are you saying Alice is willing to be with you?"

I nod. "Yes." My little bird is more than willing.

"Fine. Have we got a deal?"

I nod and hold out my hand. He glances at it skeptically before shaking. His agreement sends a wave of satisfaction through me. Thiago may be rough around the edges, but he's got influence. If he's on board, others will follow.

"Welcome to my madness."

Thiago tilts his head. "I don't think I've ever heard you speak so long without adding a riddle."

I narrow my eyes at him. "The riddles are the only thing that keeps me sane."

He laughs. "We'll agree to disagree on that. It's why everyone says you're as mad as a fucking hatter."

"What's the plan of action?" he asks.

I straighten, my eyes meeting his. "We need to gain trust within the cartel. Show them we're as ruthless and cunning as Ileana, but if they follow us, they'll get the respect and treatment they deserve."

"Some will remain loyal to her."

I nod. "Of course. But when the time is right, we take Ileana out. It won't be easy, but with enough planning and a bit of luck, we can do it."

Thiago's stony face doesn't betray his thoughts. "And what's to stop Ileana from killing us before we get close?"

"I'm her most trusted subordinate. She won't suspect me."

"And if she does?" Thiago's voice is as cold as steel, mirroring the uncertainty that creeps into my mind.

I shrug, trying to appear nonchalant. "Then we die," I reply. "But it's a risk we have to take. For Luna. For Alice. And for all of us who've been living under her tyranny for far too long."

Thiago considers this for a moment. Then, he nods, the ghost of a grim smile playing on his lips. "You're as mad as a hatter for this plan, but I'm with you." His jaw clenches. "Now, I've got to convince Matias."

"Right, he might be tough to convince considering our altercation yesterday."

His eyes narrow. "Yeah, that was a dumb move."

"He hit Alice, so I gave him what he deserved."

A flicker of rage ignites in Thiago's eyes. "I don't think he'll ever want to team up with you."

I shrug. "I'm sure you'll find a way to convince him."

Thiago grunts, leaning back in his chair as if the world's weight has landed on his shoulders. "I'll try for Luna's sake." He rubs his temples. "This is real fucking dangerous. But for some twisted reason, I believe in you." He pushes off the dresser. "I'll talk to Matias. But remember this," he points the finger at me, "If this goes south, if Luna and Alice get caught in the crossfire, it's on you."

The path ahead will be fraught with danger and uncertainty, but with Thiago and Matias on my side, I feel a glimmer of hope. "To overthrowing Ileana."

He nods in response, and I leave the room, feeling lighter than I've felt in years. I've got my first ally on my quest to cut down the Red Queen.

21

TAREN

*L*ittle does Ileana know that her insistence that I meet with Damien Vasquez will backfire on her. While I had to cancel the Estrada meeting, as this meeting clashed, Vasquez's help could be just as valuable. And Ileana sent me to him.

He's going to be my second ally after Thiago. Someone outside the Navarro cartel. I don't care about power, not really. All I care about is getting free from Ileana's oppressive rule over my life and work. And most importantly, freeing Alice. And Damien Vasquez wants her gone almost as badly as I do.

The tension cuts through me like a knife as I'm led through the towering gates of the Vasquez compound. Though littered with vines and aged by time, the ominous stone walls still reek of power and dominance.

I'm ushered down a long, extravagantly embellished corridor and into an office that's more of a monument to opulence than a workspace. The room is huge, suffocatingly so, and in the center sits Damien. As I enter, he's perched on the edge of his desk, a predatory grin spreading across his face. The tension in the room is palpable, almost alive, as we lock eyes. A twisted cocktail of anticipation and dread churns in my gut. This is the moment of truth.

"Taren, this is a surprise," he says, breaking the silence. He nods at his men. "Leave us."

"Damien," I acknowledge, my voice steady despite the storm brewing within. I take a seat, uninvited, across from him. "We need to talk about Ileana."

His jaw clenches. "What about her? I told you I'm not meeting with her, and if you'd asked, I'd have told you I wouldn't meet with you either. And yet, here you are."

"You're going to want to hear me out."

He arches a brow. "I don't like people telling me what I'm going to want." He clenches his fists. "You come in here without invitation and have the audacity to sit across from me and—"

"We both want Ileana gone," I cut in.

That stops his rant in its tracks. "What?"

"You heard me. I think we can be powerful allies to each other." I lean forward, elbows resting on my knees, my voice dropping to a conspiratorial whisper. "But Ileana, she's like a hat without a head, a boat without a sea, a key without a lock. Can't you see it?" I chuckle. "We need to be the hands that tip the teapot, the wave that capsizes the boat, the foot that squashes the hat. We need to be the end of Ileana."

He bursts into laughter. "Taren," he finally says, shaking his head. "You're a crazy son of a bitch. Why on earth would I want to ally myself with a madman? You march into my office, uninvited, and propose a revolution? Just like that?" His eyes glint with a dangerous sort of amusement. "Give me one good reason why I should take you seriously, let alone help you overthrow Ileana."

I lean back in the worn leather chair. "Because, Damien," I answer, my voice cold, "I'm the only one crazy enough to do it. And you," I point an accusing finger at him, "you're just bored enough to want to see me try." I can feel my blood pulsating through my veins, the adrenaline making everything around me seem sharper. "Believe me, I'm serious about this. Dead serious. And you hate Ileana almost as much as I do."

He smirks then. "So, it's true, then. The rumors?"

I freeze. "What rumors?"

"The rumors that she treats you like a plaything. Her little boy toy, even though she makes you call her mother."

I snap then, my resolve crashing as I stand and grab his throat, looming over the older cartel leader. "Watch your mouth, Vasquez," I growl.

He doesn't seem fazed, laughing. "Calm down, Taren. I hardly think this is the way to win my alliance, is it?"

He's pushing my buttons, and he finds it amusing. "Then don't push me."

"Fine, I admit your proposal is intriguing."

I release his throat and sit back in the chair, trying to calm the rage flooding my veins. He's clearly entertained by this whole debacle, his eyes dancing with amusement. "So, you're in?" I ask.

He smirks, shrugging nonchalantly. "Can't promise anything, but I'm interested. I want to see how this all plays out."

Noncommittal bastard. I expected as much. He won't take a risk until he's sure of the reward.

His eyes meet mine, a glint of something akin to respect in their depths. "I'll await your call."

I nod, my heart hammering in my chest. Getting

Damien on my side was a vital piece of the puzzle. "I have to report back to Ileana about this meeting." I tilt my head. "She wanted to broker a deal to make an alliance between the Vasquez Cartel and the Navarro Cartel."

Damien snorts. "Then she's even crazier than you." He shakes his head. "I'd rather eat my eyeballs than ever work with that snake. I know what she did to Gutierrez when he allied with her."

The Gutierrez Cartel used to be a formidable enemy, but Ileana double-crossed him and fed him to the sharks. Literally, she made his whole family watch before murdering them all in cold blood. This was some years ago when I was only little. However, the descriptions I've heard from some men who witnessed it make it sound like a horror film.

"At least you've got the sense to refuse; I'll tell her as much." I clench my jaw. "I don't really think she expected I'd broker a deal. However, she's convinced the Estrada Cartel is trying to secure Mexico City."

A flash of something enters Damien's eyes, but it's gone as quickly. He knows they're trying to broker a deal. Perhaps he's in on it. Is it possible he, too, is working to immobilize Ileana tactically rather than physically?"

"You already knew that," I murmur.

"I don't know what you're talking about," he says.

I smirk. "Lies are a bit like shadows, wouldn't you agree?" I meet his gaze steadily. "They're always stretching and shrinking, depending on the light. But when night falls, they're nowhere to be seen. Or maybe they're everywhere."

His jaw clenches. "You're as mad as people say."

"I'd rather be mad than dead," I mutter, as it's the only way I could survive this long. "Tell me what you know."

Damien crosses his arms over his chest. "Are you commanding me, hatter?"

I clear my throat. "It's Taren. I don't appreciate the nickname."

He shakes his head. "Estrada and I are working to secure Mexico City to rid the country of Ileana."

I smirk. "My way is probably easier, no?"

He nods. "It'd be quicker, that's for sure. And cheaper."

"So we have a deal? You'll help me when the time comes."

He nods in response. "Yes, I'll await your call. You have my word."

"Good." I clap my hands. "Enjoy the rest of your day. I'll show myself out." I turn around to leave the room.

Damien clears his throat behind me. "Be careful, Taren. You may think you know the monster you're dealing with, but the problem is she knows you, too."

I'm all too aware that Ileana can read me well. She's known me since I was eight. It's part of the reason I've adopted my riddles. If you speak in riddles, everyone thinks you're mad, but that's the method of deception.

Ileana can't learn my true intent. She needs to believe I'm a madman when really I'm driven to the brink of sanity by her treatment. And people driven to the brink are wildly unpredictable.

TAREN

J return to the house to find Jorge waiting for me.

"It's about time," he chides, sneering. "Ileana wants to see you."

I sigh heavily. "Can't even get back into the house before being given orders," I say to him, holding his gaze. "Is that how Ileana's second in command should be treated?"

Jorge's temple throbs, as he hates that I'm above him in rank. "No, sir. I'm simply relaying information."

I know it kills him to call me sir. And despite wanting nothing more than to take a shower and decompress after that meeting I had yesterday, I know better than to refuse an audience with the Red Queen.

I stride toward Ileana's office, the sound of my

boots echoing ominously in the hallway. On entering, I find her alone, pacing back and forth like a madwoman.

I clear my throat. "You summoned me?" I ask.

Her dark eyes cut to me. "You've been gone a long time. I started to worry."

I almost laugh, but keep a mask over my emotions. Ileana doesn't worry about anything but herself. "It's not a quick journey to the other side of the country," I retort.

Her nostrils flare as she sits down. "So, what happened?"

"I told Vasquez about the proposed alliance," I begin, leaning back against the threshold of the door, arms crossed. "He refused."

Although he agreed to my proposal to cut you down.

I push the thought away. My mind is getting more chaotic the longer this goes on. I need to strike soon or I fear I'll lose everything.

Ileana's eyes flash with anger and her fists clench. "What?" she snarls, teeth gritted. "That arrogant fool! He takes one look at our proposal and tosses it aside like it's nothing!" She slams her palms on the desk, causing the neatly stacked files to scatter. "He'll regret this. Soon enough, he'll realize the mistake he's made."

"He didn't give exact reasons," I say, maintaining my casual stance. "Just said he trusts his instincts. And his instincts told him to decline." I can't tell her that Vasquez already has a deal with Estrada, and now me. I can't tell her that he laughed when I told him about her proposition. "I tried to convince him, but the man won't budge."

Ileana's eyes narrow and she drums her fingers on her desk. "What about the possibility of him being in cahoots with Estrada over this deal in Mexico City?" she asks, her voice cold and calculating.

"I didn't bring it up," I reply evenly. "Didn't want to give away our cards yet."

She nods, seemingly satisfied with my answer. "Good thinking," she says with a hint of admiration in her voice. "But we need to do something soon. If they take Mexico City—"

"They won't."

She arches a brow. "So sure?"

"It's not possible no matter how much real estate they buy."

She shrugs. "I don't care if it's possible or not. I want to stop them both in their tracks."

I shake my head. "So you're assuming Vasquez is in leagues with Estrada?"

"Why else wouldn't he agree to our deal?"

Because you're a crazy psycho who always stabs her allies in the back.

"A puzzle of the mind's depths, veiled by a mysterious haze. Can one truly fathom the secrets others hold?"

She sighs and pinches the bridge of her nose. "I don't have the strength to deal with your cryptic questions." By the way, I did speak with Gaston and he confirmed that I almost lost the sale because Matias was being too forceful with the girls." Her jaw clenches. "I apologize for doubting you." She clears her throat. "But I need you back on the job again from tomorrow."

I raise a brow. "You're putting me in charge?"

She nods.

I feel relief that I'm finally going to be in control of Alice's training again. It may have only been a couple of days since she kicked me off the team, but it's driven me crazy.

"The girls need to be ready in three days time. The auction is set and invitations went out this morning."

"I see," I say, my voice coming out colder than I intend. That's faster than normal. "They've not been training for very long, what's the rush?"

She shrugs, "There's an opportunity, and I intend to seize it." Her eyes are hard, devoid of any emotion.

"The bidders are hungry. They always are. And we need the space in the prison if we're going to take on Vasquez and Estrada."

I almost retort that one cell won't make any difference, but I hold my tongue.

"Get the girls ready in three days, Taren. This is happening."

I nod in response. "Fine."

"And you know the protocol for night before. And since there's three of you and three of them, you can each have one to prepare."

I clear my throat, knowing Alice won't like that. She won't have a problem with spending the night with me, but knowing her friends are with Thiago and Matias... I'll have to handle her anger. She'll hate me for it.

"Right," I say, my tone sharper than intended. Ileana's orders echo in my mind, a haunting melody of betrayal and uneasy anticipation. I'm aware of the precarious balance I'll have to uphold, maintaining Alice's trust while ensuring the deal goes through. "I'll ensure they're primed for the auction." And that I'm ready to chop your head off, Red Queen.

Breaking these shackles, it isn't about physical restraints. It's about breaking free from the mental chains that she has put on my mind. It's a game of stealth and strategy, of trusting the right people and knowing when to strike. And the Red Queen has moved her chess piece, forcing my hand. It's a dance in the shadows, where every move could either shatter the chains or tighten them. And for Alice, for the girls, I'll become the master of this dance.

"Good. You're dismissed."

I turn away and walk out of her office. The countdown has begun. Time to break the chains of oppression that have held me down for far too many years.

And then, once we're all free. I've got a Brown University professor to massacre.

Freedom, after all, isn't given. It's taken. And I am ready to take it, to shatter these chains and to bathe in the light that is Alice after bathing in the blood of my enemies.

23

ALICE

I haven't seen Taren in a couple of days. Since then, our training has taken a rather odd turn. Matias is still his crazy, untamable self, but Thiago acts like the protector Taren once was. He's keeping his brother at bay, and they've not touched us sexually since Taren came to tell me that Ileana had pulled him off training.

Matias and Thiago have us standing on one leg as a task to see how long we'll do as we're told. Both of them sneering at us. Luna has been uncharacteristically quiet the past few days. I think it's because of what happened to Blake. We're all still shaken over it, completely unaware of what she's going through with her new owner.

Suddenly, Luna's leg buckles under her, and she nearly falls over.

Matias sneers, "Can't even do a simple task, huh?" He moves forward with violent intent in his eyes.

Before he can move toward her, Thiago steps in front of him, his arm outstretched. "That's enough, Matias," he commands, his voice firm. The air in the room turns icy as he stands his ground, preventing his brother from harming Luna.

Matias's pupils dilate, his jaw clenches, and he whirls around to face his brother. "Enough?" he spits out the word as if it's poison. "Since when do you decide what's enough, Thiago? You're suddenly playing the hero now, pretending to be Taren. Do you think that makes you better than me?"

His nostrils flare, his chest heaving with barely suppressed rage.

Thiago doesn't back down. He holds his brother's gaze, unflinching. The tension thickens in the room, a storm about to break loose.

Their confrontation escalates. "You think stepping in for Luna makes you better, huh? You're just another pawn in their game!" His fists clench at his sides, his body rigid with fury.

Thiago's face hardens, but his voice remains steady, "It's about ensuring we treat the assets correctly. No one wants to pay top dollar for a girl with bruises on her face." He looks back at Luna for a fraction of a second, a brief flicker of concern flashing across his face.

"Right?" Matias laughs bitterly, "Right according to whom, Thiago? We've been doing this for years, and suddenly that bastard Taren turns up, and everything changes."

Thiago bristles at his brother's words, but he stands his ground, his eyes unwavering. The tension is palpable, the room heavy with unspoken animosity, and the impending storm continues to brew.

"Enough," Taren's voice cuts through the silence.

The relief of hearing his voice is unlike anything I've ever felt. I turn to face him, but he doesn't look at me. His gaze is fixed on the two brothers.

"I need to speak with you both," he demands, still focusing on them.

I expect him to look at me, but he doesn't. Instead, he turns away and walks out of view of the cell, expecting the brothers to follow. To my surprise, they do follow him. No questions.

Luna glances at me. "Something's going on."

I bite my lip. "Maybe."

Kali approaches, her eyes still glassy from tears. "I hate Matias."

"You and me both," I say.

The sound of muffled voices echo toward the cell. I hate that I've got no idea what's happening, but something is off.

I stand there, feeling the cold seep into the very marrow of my bones. The uncertainty gnawing at me worse than the cold.

"Are you alright?" Luna asks, placing a hand on my arm. "You're shaking."

I swallow hard. "I sense that something big is going to happen."

Luna pulls me close, and Kali joins the hug, all of us seeking comfort in each other. The absence of Blake feels more poignant in that moment.

"God, I hope Blake is okay," Kali mutters.

My stomach churns as I try not to dwell on what she's going through. The unease is an icy hand around my heart, tightening with every passing second. Kali's eyes are wide and frightened. Luna's are hardened and unyielding but filled with a shared dread.

"I hate this," Kali whispers, her voice barely audible.

"I know," Luna responds, her hand still on my arm, radiating a foreign warmth in this cold place.

"The unknown," I murmur, breaking the silence.

"That's what's driving us insane. Not knowing what's happening. What's going to happen."

Luna nods, her lips drawn into a thin line. "We need to be prepared for whatever comes next."

I force a smile. "Easier said than done."

Taren reappears, his face inscrutable, flanked by Matias and Thiago. They all look like shadows, their faces hard and unreadable in the dim light. "I'm training you again, but not for long," Taren announces, his voice bouncing off the walls.

A mix of relief and unease pulse through me.

"In three days, you'll be put up for auction in front of the rich and powerful of Mexico," he announces, eyes fixated on me.

He's trying to tell me something. Is this all part of his plan? I hope it is.

"Which means you need to be on your best behavior," Thiago adds, his gaze on Luna.

Luna, surprisingly, bows her head in response.

Matias' is focused on Kali, who meets his gaze. She's been so subservient since we got here. "Good, anyone who will buy me will be better than you," she says, all her focus on him.

Matias growls and stalks forward, reacting instantly to Kali's words. His face twists into a snarl, his eyes flaring with a wild, dangerous heat. He looks at Kali not as a predator eyeing its prey but as a man possessed. "No one else touches you," he growls, his voice a low rumble.

And then he grabs her throat, casting a shadow over her. The message is clear, but it's not possible. He's staking his claim and marking his territory, which is Kali.

"Back off, brother. Unless you've got millions of dollars to buy her, someone else will be touching her."

Matias growls and releases her, spinning on his brother.

Taren steps toward him. "Control yourself," he demands, glaring at Matias, whose face is still bruised after the beating Taren put him through for touching me.

Matias snarls but backs down. He goes to stand by his brother but doesn't take his gaze off Kali.

"Now resume balancing on one foot," Taren instructs.

His jaw is hard set, and tension coils through his body. He's not at ease as he usually is, and it shows. It puts me on edge, but I do as I'm told and balance. My eyes fixated on him as he avoids meeting my gaze. All I want to know is what's going on. How is he going to get us out of this auction?

Luna slips again, and Taren growls. "How are we

supposed to sell you if you can't even follow simple instructions." His jaw works, and a vein protrudes on his forehead. I wonder if he'll strike her, but he controls himself.

"Again," he barks.

Luna glares at him as she moves back into position. It kills holding it like this, my thighs aching.

The following silence is thick and heavy, filled with unspoken words and inexpressible frustrations.

Taren's gaze is still averted, his cold exterior an impenetrable wall. I

feel my heart sink into the pit of my stomach.

He has a plan. He must have. But his silence and frigid dismissal leave me feeling more uncertain and alone than ever. I watch as his gaze flickers briefly toward me before skirting away. That small action, so out of character, sends a shiver down my spine.

Is he giving up?

Does he even care anymore?

I can't shake off the sinking feeling. The uncertainty of our future looms over us like a dark cloud, casting a chilling shadow on what was left of our hope.

24
TAREN

*A*lice watches me as I pace around my bedroom. Her gaze an ever-present reminder of the rules I'm breaking, but tomorrow is D-Day. And I need to drown in my little bird tonight. Explore this undeniable connection that we share.

"What's going on?" Alice asks.

I stop and look at her, as I've had to keep her in the dark these past two days. "The auction is tomorrow."

"I know, and are you going to stop it?"

I nod. "Tomorrow. A day when the skies bleed crimson and the earth shivers in anticipation. A ballet of power where the pawns and kings are indistinguishable. That, little bird, is what awaits us."

Her brow furrows. "What?"

"I'm going to kill her tomorrow," I say simply.

Her jaw falls open. "Just like that."

I nod. "Just like that."

"How are you intending to explain taking me out of the cell?"

My jaw clenches. "Tomorrow is the auction where you're supposed to be sold. Ileana unwittingly requested that each of us 'break' you in."

She freezes. "Are you saying Luna and Kali are..."

I nod. "I'm afraid so. I'm sorry, little bird, there was nothing I could—"

"Bullshit." Her jaw clenches. "Stop saying there's nothing you can do." She rushes toward me, anger in her eyes. "Help them!" She beats her fist against my chest.

I grab her wrist. "You dare command me?" I growl, yanking her closer. Her surprise is palpable, her defiance sparking a strange thrill within me. "You forget your place, Alice." Roughly, I flip her around, pressing her against the bed. "Perhaps you need a reminder."

She struggles beneath me, her futile resistance only fueling my anger. "Let me go!" she cries, her voice muffled by the mattress.

"Haven't you figured it out yet?" I snarl, my hand landing sharply against her rear. "I may intend to free you from here, but you'll never be free of me. You belong to me," I growl, unable to bring my rage out of control.

Everything I've done for her. All the work I've put in. And she's acting like a fucking brat. A brat that needs to be taught a lesson.

"I'm not your savior, Alice. I'm another monster in your nightmare."

Her cries echo in the room, a haunting melody that feeds my fury. "Stop!" she pleads, but I don't relent. Each smack is a reminder of who I am really.

My hand lands again, and she gasps, her body trembling beneath me. "Taren, please," she whimpers. Even as she tries to hide it, her voice is laced with desire.

Her fantasy from before graces my mind.

I imagine you tearing me apart roughly while I tell you to stop, and all the while, I love every second.

My dirty little bird.

"Silence," I command, spanking her once more. "If you really want this to stop, then say the safe word."

She shudders. "What is it?"

"Wonderland," I say.

And then I stop, leaving her gasping and trembling on the bed from my punishment. For a few moment, I take in the image of her ass red from my beatings, relishing the sight. And then I flip her over on the bed and push up her dress, finding her cunt soaking wet.

"See, Alice," I breathe. "This is what you asked for, isn't it? You, beneath me, begging me to stop." My fingers trail down her wetness and she gasps, the sound turning into a whimper as I taste her on my fingers. "And yet, your body betrays you, doesn't it? You're soaking wet for me, baby." I smirk as I trace a path along her thigh with my fingers. "Do you feel how much you want me, Alice?" I purr, my fingers slipping inside her, her hips bucking against my hand. "You might say 'stop', but your body says 'more'." I chuckle. "Your words say no, but your cunt says yes. And who am I to deny what it wants?" I move lower, my tongue exploring her, tasting her, relishing in the sweet, decadent flavour of her desire.

"You wanted the monster, Alice," I remind her, my fingers curling inside her, my tongue lapping at her clit. "And now you have him," I growl, my voice a dangerous purr. "So tell me to stop, Alice. Beg me to stop," I challenge, my eyes locked onto hers, my fingers pumping inside her. "Because, every time you do, it just makes me want you more."

The fire in her eyes is ablaze now. She's lost to the sensation.

"Stop!" She fights against me hard. Her body

arching against my hand as she tries to escape. I hold firm and grab her throat, squeezing hard enough to partially block her airways and to leave bruises around her neck like a collar. "But there's no stopping now, Alice," I say, my voice a resonating growl that fills the room.

Despite her feeble protests, I continue my relentless assault, my fingers working their magic inside her, bringing her closer and closer to the edge.

Her body betrays her pleas, her wetness telling me all I need to know. Her resistance fuels me, spurring me on. She may be begging for mercy, but her body craves more. "You wanted this," I smirk, feeling her body trembling beneath me. "This is your fantasy, isn't it?"

Her eyes flash at that, but she doesn't reply.

I can't contain myself any longer. Feeling her teetering on the brink shreds my remaining restraint. I pull my hand free, hastily shrugging out of my pants. But as soon as she feels the shift, Alice tries to bolt. She squirms out from beneath me, a dash for the bathroom.

"Where do you think you're flying off to, little bird?"

Alice draws in a deep, shuddering breath as I yank her against me. "Taren, I don't understand."

"Understand what?" I ask, unzipping the back of her dress to remove it.

I can feel the tension coiling through her. "Why you wouldn't just fuck me before when I begged you. Why wait until now?"

She wants to turn around, but I don't let her. Instead, I allow the tattered, dirty fabric of her dress to drop to the floor. "Because tomorrow is our reckoning. Because I'm not in control of this plan. And if I die tomorrow, I know I will die unfulfilled if I don't claim you."

Her breath hitches at my words. The rhythm of our dance suddenly shifts, taking on a less sinister air.

"Taren," she whispers, her voice a mix of uncertainty and longing. "How likely is it you'll succeed?"

I'm a rational, logical man, even if most wouldn't believe it. And I've gone over the odds a hundred times. They've split right down the middle. Ileana moving the auction up so quick has forced me into a corner.

"It's a possibility," I admit, turning her around to gaze into those sky-blue eyes. "But tonight," I whisper, my voice husky. "Tonight, we're going to fulfil that little fantasy of yours." The words hang heavy between us as my fingers trace patterns on her bare skin. Her breath catches, and I smirk, savoring the anticipation.

"Daisy," I say, turning her to face me. "That'll be your safe word. If things go too far, if you need me to stop — say 'Daisy'. Do you understand, Alice?" I scrutinize her, searching for any sign of fear or reluctance in her eyes.

She nods, a strand of hair falling down to obscure her view. Her cheeks are flushed, her breath quickening. "Daisy," she repeats, her voice soft but steady.

I can see the trust in her eyes, the desire, the fear. I know she's prepared, as much as she can be. I'm going to give her the night she dreamed of if it's the last thing I do on this earth.

Slowly, I pull out the ropes and balaclava from the drawer, laying them out one by one on the bed. The sight of them causes her to shiver, but her gaze never leaves mine. I reach out, brushing her hair back from her eyes. "Are you sure about this, little bird?" I ask.

"Yes," she breathes out.

I grab the balaclava and slip it over my head. "You trust a madman with the deepest corners of your psyche, Alice," I murmur, the words muffled slightly by the balaclava. "You're giving me the keys to your darkest desires, entrusting me with your vulnerabilities." I run a gloved finger down her cheek, watching as she swallows hard, her eyes never leaving mine. "It's a fascinating paradox, isn't it? So delicate, so fragile, yet you hand it over willingly to someone as unhinged as me. You're playing with fire, little bird. But remember, even the most mesmerizing flames can leave you scorched."

"Taren," she whispers my name.

I grab her forcefully and push her onto her back on the bed, wrapping her wrists with the ropes, binding them tight enough to hurt but not too tight to cut her circulation. And then I affix them to the bed posts, restraining her at my mercy.

I step back to admire the view, her bound on the bed, her breathing heavy as her bare chest rises and falls. Her breasts are pure perfection, nipples hard and pointed right at me. I want to suck on them. But for now, I'm enjoying her fear and anticipation.

"You're a twisted little thing, aren't you?" I ask, my voice rippling with dark amusement. "Bound and yet free, scared and yet excited. You're the perfect paradox and I can't help but dive into your complexities."

Her eyes flash with a wild desire. "Taren," she pleads. "Please don't..."

I nod, acknowledging her, and move forward. "You're flying high, aren't you, little bird?" I whisper.

"No, please stop this. I don't—"

I start forward and cut her off with a firm hand around her throat, glaring down at her. The force of my desire is confusing. This woman. She's brought me to my knees. I truly have lost my mind.

"I'm going to tear you apart. And I'm going to love every second. And the more you fight. The more you say no, the harder my fucking dick gets. Did you know that, baby? Did you know you're dealing with a man this perverse?"

She can't reply because I'm blocking her airway.

I release it just long enough to finish removing my pants and then my shirt.

Alice gasps when she sees the burns on my chest. It's the first time I've bared myself to her. "Wha—"

I place my hand over her mouth. "Not now," I growl, my cock hard and throbbing against her soaking cunt. "You're going to take my cock and enjoy it, little bird."

I move over her, pinning her down with my weight. "You're a feisty one, aren't you?" I murmur, my gaze fixated on the fear flashing in her eyes. But it's not just fear; there's an undercurrent of excitement, of anticipation. And that excites me, sends a thrill coursing down my spine. I reach for the zipper of her jeans, slowly dragging it down.

"Please... don't..." she stammers, but I pay no heed.

I lean down, pressing my lips to her ear. "You know what's so damn intoxicating about you, Alice?" I hiss, my fingers trailing over the soft fabric of her panties. "It's that you're scared, yet so fucking aroused. You don't want this, but your body is begging for my touch."

She whimpers as I slide my hand into her panties, her body trembling beneath me. Alice's hips jerk and she pulls at the restraints as I tear her panties off and discard them. "Stop," she grits out.

I lower my mouth to hers but don't kiss her. "This is what you get for being a dirty little bird." I slam my cock inside her with one stroke, making her scream.

"You know how to stop me," I challenge, my voice a raspy growl. Even as I say the words, I don't know that I could stop. Her cunt feels like heaven around my dick. "Say the word and I will." I know she won't. Because she wants this just as much as I do.

Her gaze doesn't waver as my cock stretches her. "Don't do this!"

I laugh, a harsh, bitter sound that echoes through the room. "Begging already, love?" I taunt, my voice dripping with cruel amusement. "I thought you liked it rough." I thrust into her again, harder this time, drinking in the gasping breaths she sucks in. "Is it too much for you, Alice?" I lean in close, my lips brushing against her ear. "Do you want me to stop?"

I can feel her body trembling, her muscles clamping down on me in a way that drives me wild.

One word and everything stops.

She doesn't respond, and I let out a soft chuckle. "Didn't think so," I murmur. With a slow withdrawal, I plunge back into her, her moans of pain and pleasure blending together. "You enjoy it, don't you?" I gasp, my voice strained. "Being fucked like a dirty little bird by a monster like me."

Our dance continues, each thrust creating a symphony of sounds from Alice's lips—a mix of agony and ecstasy. Her body writhes beneath me, yearning for more. Her silent surrender only fuels my desire. I can't stop, won't stop, until I've claimed every inch of her. Alice is mine and the only way Ileana is selling her to another tomorrow is over my dead fucking body.

25
ALICE

*T*aren's eyes look black in the dim light of the room as he keeps the balaclava over his head. I run my hands down his burned skin, wondering what happened to him. He's tortured in so many ways. The scars remind me of his childhood home ravaged by flames.

Did Ileana burn him?

What darkness lurks in his past, driving him?

I moan as he slams into me again, my hips rising to meet his actions. "Taren, stop," I groan, trying to keep playing my part in our twisted act.

It's what I wanted. Taren is the first man I've allowed inside me since Michael raped me. And yet my fucked up mind wants to play it out. As if it's the only way to wrap my head around the trauma.

"You like this, don't you?" His words are a guttural growl against my ear. A hot whisper that sends shivers down my spine. "My dirty little bird likes getting raped."

I grind my teeth, my mind and body at war. I know it's wrong. I know it doesn't make sense. Yet, there's a twisted logic to it, a sensation of control amidst the chaos. I can stop it if I want. But I don't. One word, and our fantasy shatters.

Taren continues. His rhythm unrelenting. His grip tightens around my hair, pulling my head back to expose my neck. "You wanted this. Needed this."

He's right.

I arch my back as he fucks me so deep I don't know where I end, and he begins. "No," I spit. "Stop!" I keep playing my part, making his eyes flash. He goes harder, and it hurts and feels good all at the same time.

We both know I've got the word to stop this. And I won't use it because this is what I need. Taren and his madness are like balm for my broken soul. And I want to drown in him. I want him to take my broken pieces and put them back together with his.

"I can see the fear in your eyes, but there's excitement, too. Admit it." He leans toward my ear, the fabric of the balaclava brushing my skin. "And, little bird, I get off on fear. It's fucking intoxicating." I feel him fumble with something beneath the pillow under my head. And then he pulls out a blade, glinting dangerously in the low light.

"What—"

He uses his other hand to cover my mouth. The cool metal of the blade presses against my skin, a shock of fear and anticipation arcing me. "You didn't know how dark I could be, did you?"

A tremor of uncertainty courses through me. There's a primal part of me, a part I didn't know existed until tonight, that thrills at the sight of the blade. Yet another part of me recoils. There's a flutter of fear running up my spine, making my heart pound like a jackhammer in my chest.

A twisted smile forms on his lips as he traces the blade over my skin. It's not hard enough to draw blood merely scraping it. "I see you flinch when the blade touches your soft skin, but I also see the excitement in your eyes. You're playing with fire." He maneuvers the blade and presses it slightly to let a tiny droplet of blood surface. "My fire is unlike any you've encountered before. It won't just burn you, it'll consume you."

His gaze is locked on mine, a dark hunger in his eyes as he lowers his mouth to my skin.

I gasp as he licks the blood and then sucks, tasting it like a heathen beast.

He lifts his eyes to mine, practically black now. "You taste perfect. My dark and twisted drug." He grins, a flash of white against the darkness, and raises the blade again. His hand is steady, the glinting steel poised above my skin. "Now," he murmurs, "to add my mark to ensure everyone knows you belong to me. T.C."

My breath catches as the blade dances across my skin, carefully sculpting the letters, the sharp sting cutting through the haze of pleasure. "What does the 'C' stand for?" I ask through gritted teeth as he finishes his work.

"Castillo," he responds, his voice rough with emotion. "My birth name. Ileana changed it to Navarro." A shadow passes over his features, but it's gone as quickly as it came.

They call him the mad hatter, and I love that about him. The madness is what drew me to him the moment we met.

I know I'm marked, claimed. His initials on my skin are a testament to our twisted bond. And strangely, I find myself not only accepting it, but craving it. Taren Castillo. The man has inscribed himself onto my being, not just my skin. He's deep in my soul, so deep I couldn't ever get him out.

"Your blood is as intoxicating as the finest wine." He runs the edge of the blade across his tongue, licking my blood from it. "Do you feel that? Your life force is mingling with mine."

I shudder, but my arousal increases. "I don't know what I feel. All I know is I've never wanted anything more than you."

He drops the knife to the ground and groans, kissing me. The metallic taste of my blood still lingers on his tongue, and I'm shocked that the taste only drives me higher. My desire is becoming so intense it feels like it will destroy me. And then he thrusts again, harder and faster. Our bodies come together in a clash of skin against skin.

I pull at the restraints around my wrists, the rope chaffing my skin. A moan tumbles from my lips as the depravity drives me wild. I'm broken, and yet it feels like Taren is the key to fixing me. Or maybe he's just the only person who's seen the real me. The broken and fucked up me, and he's accepting it.

"You're a naughty little bird, aren't you?" Taren growls into my ear, sending a thrill through my veins. "Do you like that? Being tied up, at my mercy? Being cut and branded?" His words ignite something within me, a primal desire.

He slams into me with long, slow, and hard strokes. "Say it," he urges. "Say you're mine." He smiles against the skin on my neck. "Say that I'm the only man that will ever be inside you again."

I gasp. All the air leaves my body in a sudden rush. My pulse quickens, my heart beating like a wild drum. I look into his eyes, which are dark with desire and wild possession. And at that moment, I know I belong to this man. Not just my body but my soul as well. It's terrifying and exhilarating.

"Yes," I admit, my voice a whisper. I swallow hard, my throat suddenly dry. "Yes, Taren. You own me. My body, my soul, all of it." I drag my fingers down his scarred, tattooed skin. "You, and only you. Always."

He growls and then kisses me, fucking me harder and faster. I moan, my hips lifting from the bed to meet each thrust. Our movements synchronize as our connection becomes raw, animalistic, and unlike anything I'd ever known.

His lips are rough and demanding against mine, his tongue exploring the depths of my mouth as if he's claiming every inch of me.

"I love hearing you say that," he murmurs between

thrusts, his gaze never leaving mine. "You're mine, all mine."

I can feel the strength of his conviction, his need to make me feel loved and cherished. We may not have admitted our feelings out loud, but we don't need to. I feel it in the way he looks at me.

I respond to his thrusts with abandon, my nails digging into his back as wave after wave of pleasure washes over me.

"You're my good girl, aren't you?"

"Yes," I gasp, my voice full of raw desire. "Always your good girl." Each word from his mouth stirs a hunger within me that only he can satisfy.

His growl of approval is primal. The dark possession in his gaze stirs a thrilling sense of fear and excitement. A potent combination that leaves me breathless. He kisses a path from my neck to my collarbone, each press of his lips a branding mark, a claim that I'm his and his alone.

And then his teeth sink into my collarbone, the pain spiking the pleasure. I've felt this sense of loneliness all my life, but with him I feel safe, protected and whole.

My heart pounds in my chest, our bodies moving together aggressively. The faint scent of his cologne fills my senses, a heady mix of musk and spice unique to Taren.

"You're mine," he repeats, his voice a low rumble against my ear. "Only mine, Alice. Remember that." His words, possessive and powerful, strike a chord within me.

His movements become more deliberate. Each thrust is a testament to his control and restraint.

I grip his shoulders, back arching as he hits the right spot. "Taren, please," I beg, my voice a broken plea. The world spins, pleasure surging through me like a wave, intense and unrelenting.

"Come for me," he demands. "I want your tight little cunt to milk my cock," he growls.

"Fuck!" I cry as an unparalleled pleasure spirals through me. It feels like I'm free-falling. It's an explosive force, a blinding light devouring every corner of my consciousness. This moment. Our coupling has been a long time coming. Or at least, it has felt like it since I was captured. But I'm sure only a couple of weeks have passed.

"Good girl," he praises, and then he thrusts once more before growling and coming. His cock slamming into me with so much force it's like he's trying to break me apart, draining every drop.

I'm thankful at that moment that I've got an IUD

fitted, as Taren didn't even mention birth control. I had it fitted after the encounter two years ago with Michael because I wasn't on any and had to get a morning-after pill. So, I've safeguarded myself in the best way possible.

Taren stills with his forehead against mine, breathing deeply. "You're not just a woman to me, Alice. You're not just a possession. You're the universe encapsulated in this one beautiful, formidable soul." He kisses me. "My queen."

I shudder at the sentiment. He pulls out of me and then lies down, tugging me onto his chest and wrapping an arm around my shoulder.

I'm home. Taren is my home. I know I'm his, completely and utterly. Always.

26

TAREN

I pace up and down Thiago's room.

"How many are on our side?" I question.

His jaw clenches. "Fifteen."

I pause. "Fuck. How are we supposed to overthrow Ileana with only fifteen men?"

Thiago shrugs. "We'll have to make do with what we have."

He's right. We have little choice. Even with Damien Vasquez's backing, it'll be tough to overthrow Ileana. But we can't back down now. The auction is at eight o'clock tonight, and if we don't move during it, Alice and her friends will be lost to us.

"Matias is convinced?" I confirm as I know he had

trouble winning his brother over. The guy is fucked in the head far more than I ever have been.

Thiago nods. "He is."

I exhale, relieved. Matias may be unpredictable, but he's strong and loyal. I'm glad to have him on our side.

"But we need more men," I say, running my hand through my hair. "We can't take down an entire army with just fifteen."

"Maybe we don't have to take down an army," Thiago suggests.

I know what he's going to say. Cut the head of the snake. Go in with stealth. Kill Ileana, and the rest will have to fall in line. I fear trying to get that close to Ileana suddenly will alert her of my intentions. She knows me better than anyone, even if I've tried to make it difficult for her to read me.

"I can try," I finally concede, looking into Thiago's eyes. "But it won't be easy. She knows me better than anyone."

Thiago's jaw clenches. "We might not survive this," he mutters.

I meet his gaze and nod. "It's a real possibility."

"Is Vasquez still on our side? Can't he provide backup?" Thiago suggests.

"He's a non-committal bastard, but I'll ask." I've had one conversation with him since our meeting, and he backpedaled a bit when I asked about support. "I'll give him a call now." I pull my cell phone out of my pocket and dial his number.

It rings three times before he answers. "Taren, what now?" he demands.

"Tonight. I need backup. Can you provide it?" I demand.

There's a few moments of silence. "You're going to kill Ileana tonight?"

I grind my teeth. "Yes, but we've only got fifteen men on our side. I need more backup. I've got a plan, but it involves your men."

He chuckles. "Of course it does."

"You can't expect to get something for free. If you want The Red Queen gone, then you help me."

He sighs. "Fine, what do you need?"

"The auction starts at eight o'clock tonight. I need you to arrive half an hour early and start shooting outside. When I go to check it out, you'll make a show of disarming me and taking me back into the auction *captured*."

"Right, and then what?" Damien presses.

"Then, your men will put me and Ileana in a cell together. There are cells at the auction house for the assets. Once I'm in there with her, I'll murder her. Just make sure you shake the bitch down for any hidden weapons."

Damien laughs. "I must admit, I thought you were a madman, but that's one of the best plans I've heard. I'm with you."

"Good," I reply.

I end the call, looking at Thiago, who had been quietly listening in. His expression is unreadable. "Well?" Thiago asks, crossing his arms over his chest.

"Damien's in," I confirm, a flicker of relief passing through me. "His men will stage a distraction at the auction and capture me and Ileana, putting us both in a cell together."

Thiago nods, taking a deep breath. "It's a good plan as long as no one fucks us over." We both know that we're gambling with high stakes here. Any of the fifteen men we've recruited could double-cross us. If that happens, Ileana will know our plan.

"We keep Damien's involvement and plan between us for now. As a backup in case someone tells Ileana."

Thiago nods. "Agreed."

"The dice of fate we've thrown into the night, will the stars of fortune shine bright? The time of reckoning is nigh, will we soar free or in darkness die?"

Thiago rolls his eyes. "I prefer it when you don't act like a mad hatter."

I laugh. "Old habits die hard," I say.

He claps me on the shoulder. "We can do this. It may be a huge task, but I believe in you and our ability to destroy her."

As Thiago's hand falls from my shoulder, I walk toward the small grimy window to my left, gazing at the cold stone courtyard below. Ileana, my oppressor, incarcerator of my sanity, the woman I've dreamt of eliminating for what feels like eons. Tonight, that dream edges closer to reality.

Fear intertwines with anticipation, a serpentine dance of dread and deliverance.

She who has stripped away my freedom, my dignity, my peace, and all the love in my life will soon meet her end. As I stand on this precipice, the taste of retribution grows sweeter. Tonight, I'll reclaim what she stole from me. Tonight, either I break my chains or become eternally bound by death. Her reign ends tonight, or I do.

27

ALICE

As we're ushered into the garishly lit auction house, I can feel the weight of dozens of eyes, each undressing us. The air is thick with expensive perfume and male cologne, a sickening combination that makes my stomach churn.

The glint of predatory anticipation in their eyes is undeniable. I look around, hoping to find Taren's familiar face among the crowd. But he's nowhere to be seen.

Luna shuffles her feet in front of me and Kali behind me. We're like cattle being herded to the slaughter. Both my friends are trembling. I can feel the shaking in our combined chains. Maybe I'm shaking too. I'm scared, but I can't let it show. We've got to be strong.

We're dressed in skimpy, see-through gowns with lingerie underneath. The outfits were chosen for us, designed to simultaneously make us look desirable and vulnerable. It's all part of the game we never wanted to play.

But as we reach the holding area, my stomach dips. A dozen guards stand around the area, staring at the three of us like we're a juicy steak on a plate.

How does Taren plan on saving us from this?

The place is guarded heavier than the prison we were taken from. One of the guards moves forward and unchains the three of us from each other. "Sit," he barks, nodding at the three wooden stools in the center of the room.

We obey without a word, perching on the stools like three birds on a wire. The guards circle us like hungry wolves. One of them, a burly man with a twisted grin, steps forward. "We've got an hour. Let's check these girls are ready."

The one who brought us here smirks. "Stand," he demands.

We comply, our movements stiff.

"Hop on one foot," the other demands.

The rest of the guards in the area chuckle. Not this again. Luna struggles to hop but does it. None of us fall as they force us to hop for what feels like hours, but it's probably only minutes.

The burly guard smirks. "Kneel," he growls.

We comply, helpless to disobey, each action stripping our dignity bit by bit.

The same guard unzips his pants, revealing himself. His eyes are on Kali as he issues his next command. "You," he says, staring at Kali. "Open your mouth."

My heart thunders in my chest. Kali's eyes widen, but she doesn't move. None of us do. We're frozen in terror. His grin widens, and I know this is just the beginning. I desperately scan the room again for any sign of Taren.

Is he really going to leave us to this fate?

Kali doesn't open her mouth.

"I said, open your fucking mouth, whore." He steps closer, his dick an inch from her mouth. "Now."

"Carlos!" Relief coils through me at the sound of that voice. Taren's voice. "What the fuck do you think you're doing?"

Carlos, the burly guard, steps back and pales. He stuffs his cock back in his pants, glancing at him sheepishly. "Wanted to make sure the girls are ready."

Taren steps forward, his gaze searing holes through

Carlos. "That's not your job," he says. "I've already made sure they're ready." His dark, almost black eyes sweep over us, a flash of concern crossing his features. It's gone as quickly as it appears. He's still playing his part.

"To your stations," Taren commands the guards, his voice echoing around the room. They disperse immediately, leaving us alone with him.

As Taren walks toward us, I can see the anger in his eyes, but there's something else too. "Did they touch you?" he growls, eyes on mine.

I shake my head. "No," I breathe.

The tension in his muscles eases. "Good, or I would've ripped his throat out."

"I..." My voice is barely a whisper, barely heard over the distant commotion. I want to ask Taren if everything will be okay, but the answer is already in his eyes. They're hard and cold, reflecting a reality he's too afraid to put into words. He doesn't know. Not really.

I swallow hard, my throat tight and my heart heavy. Taren can't promise our safety, and he can't assure a happy ending. All we have is the silent understanding that we're in this together, no matter the outcome.

"We might die," I confirm.

His jaw clenches. "I'll do anything to save you," he whispers.

I know he can't be heard saying these things, not by anyone here. It could be fatal. "Be careful," I mutter.

Thiago appears in the doorway. "Taren, it's time."

Taren's back tenses.

Thiago's attention lingers on Luna, his jaw clenching. He doesn't say anything but looks as concerned for her as Taren looks for me. My brow furrows as he turns and leaves.

"Keep your heads down when it all goes to shit." Taren turns away and walks out of the holding area, leaving us alone.

I glance at Luna. "Is there something going on with you and Thiago?" I ask. I've been wondering about it for a while. Might as well get it out in the open if we might die.

Luna's tanned cheeks instantly flush pink. "I don't know what you're talking about," she murmurs, but her blush tells me a different story.

Maybe we're both as crazy as each other. "You like him?" I ask.

She sighs. "What the hell. I know I accused you of Stockholm Syndrome, but I've fallen into the trap, too."

Kali tenses a little by her side. "Maybe I have as well." She sounds broken.

My brow furrows. "What?"

Surely not. Matias has been fucking vile to her.

She shakes her head, hugging her arms around herself. "I don't know. I'm feeling fucked up."

I reach out and place my hand on her shoulder to offer comfort. "Kali, you don't have to figure it out now," I tell her. "We're all in strange waters here."

Luna nods, her face serious. "It's okay, Kali. We're with you, no matter what."

Kali looks at us, her eyes brimming with tears, but she doesn't respond. We settle into a somber silence, each of us lost in our thoughts. The room feels suffocating.

"Whatever happens," I say, breaking the silence. "We stick together. We fight together."

They both nod, their expressions determined. The gravity of our situation hangs over us, but there's a certain strength in our unity, a silent promise to stand by each other, come what may.

I must be strong. We all need to be. Because in this world of monsters and men, our survival depends on it.

28
TAREN

*I*leana sits on her 'throne,' A huge chair at the center of the auction house, oblivious to the storm brewing. She remains a picture of serenity, unaware of the silent blade being sharpened to sever her reign.

And I, the man who will wield that blade, stands by her right side, still playing the part of the loyal servant.

She leans toward me. "Taren, I hope you got that pretty little gringo out of your system last night. I sense she's going to fetch a healthy sum of money. After all, Manuel Beltran is here. And he loves the gringos."

I clench my jaw slightly, trying to keep a handle on my emotions. "She was never in my system."

Manuel Beltran is the worst possible man Alice

could end up serving. Ileana's trying to get a rise out of me, which is concerning. Clearly, she suspects something. What, exactly, I can't be sure.

She chuckles. "Loosen up, Taren. It's a party."

I glance at her, meeting her black gaze. "What kind of party do you go to when you're alone?"

She growls in annoyance.

"A search party," I say.

"Why do I bother with you?" she asks.

I shrug. "Because you love torture in all forms."

A slight smirk tugs at her lips. "You're correct, for once." There's something in her eyes. A warning. Is it possible she knows of my plans?

I ignore the tugging feeling that she might know my intent and try to remain as passive as possible. Ileana is a master manipulator who could easily use any information against me.

"Let the games begin," she murmurs.

I grind my teeth, knowing that I'm waiting on Damien now. He's due to pose as the distraction. But his timing needs to be perfect. If he's too late... I don't want to think about it. Once those girls are sold, the men who buy them will fight to keep their hold on them. Otherwise, they'll look weak.

It's what this life is about. Power and money. The

two things that matter and weakness can't come into the equation.

But for now, I can only wait and hope Damien Vasquez will come through. Our plan hinges on him keeping his promise and promptly attacking this event. It's a risky move, but we've got no other options.

As I anxiously wait for the signal from Damien, my mind is racing with thoughts of potential outcomes. Will we be successful in taking down Ileana? Will we all make it out alive?

But then, amid my worries, a sudden commotion breaks out. Gunshots ring through the air and chaos erupts as the game begins.

Ileana stiffens, glancing at me. "What the fuck is going on?"

I shrug, brow furrowing. "I don't know."

"Check it out, now!" she barks, looking panicked. I haven't seen her panicked many times before. If she suspects me, she didn't expect this.

I pull my gun from my belt and nod. "I'll find out what it is. Probably one of the potential buyers getting trigger-happy."

Her eyes narrow. "Sort it!" she snaps.

A lot of the buyers are looking nervous as they stand, all of them ready to bolt. I nod to a few of the men who are backing us. "You lot. Come with me." I turn to the audience, making a show. "It's nothing to worry about. Sit down and relax."

Most of the buyers don't relax. They look ready to fight.

Perfect.

This is what we need. Chaos.

I head down to the entrance, where Damien will enter. When I get there, his men are already there. To my surprise, so is he. My brow furrows. "I didn't expect you to be part of the fight," I say as I greet him.

He smirks. "And miss watching Ileana lose everything?" He shakes his head. "I wouldn't miss that for anything."

My respect for him increases. Ileana would never take the risk and be in the mix of a rebellion. "Fair enough. Let's do this."

He grabs my wrists and pulls them behind me. "You've got the knife, right?" he asks.

I nod.

"Good. Make it fucking hurt."

"I intend to." Visions of Ileana bleeding and begging for her life could my mind. The plan is that Ileana and I'll be thrown into a cell together. And then, I'll kill her. But I intend to take my time and collect her blood.

We return to the main auction room where the clamor of the unsettled crowd hits us like a wave. I glance around, posing as Damien's captured prisoner. My eyes find Ileana almost instantly. The sight that greets me is unexpected and unpleasant.

She's holding Alice with a knife pressed tight against her throat. My heart sink, but I force myself to stay calm. I can't afford to lose it now. I meet Ileana's eyes. There's a triumph in her gaze and a cruel smirk on her face. She thinks she's won. But this game isn't over yet.

The smirk drops when she sees Damien Vasquez holding me captive. And then her gaze moves briefly toward Pedro Lopez, one man who supposedly went over to our side. Thiago felt someone would betray us, so we were the only two who knew of Damien's involvement.

"Vasquez," she growls, glaring at him. "What the fuck do you think you're doing?"

"Staging a coup. You're reign on this part of Mexico is over."

She laughs. "And how exactly are you going to take me down?"

"I've got your pet," Damien says, referring to me. "And if you want him to live, you'll surrender."

I see the cogs whirring behind her eyes. She's

considering her options. The question is, does she feel attached enough to me to back down? I hate her, but she's always had this sick love for me I'll never understand. "My men outnumber you, too," he bluffs as more of her men are here.

Instead of backing down, Ileana pushes Alice forward and pulls out her gun, shooting it toward Damien.

He drops with me, both of us taking cover as chaos ensues. Machine guns going off everywhere.

"Shit," I say.

Alice fell to the floor, and when I glance back, she remains there. Sit tight, little bird. I can't get to her yet, as I must go after Ileana. It tears me up, but Thiago knows to keep the girls safe. All of them. If anything happens to Alice on his watch, I'll murder him.

"Shit is right," Damien replies, eyes narrowing. "She doesn't hold enough importance to your life to surrender."

"Clearly," I reply, although I expected that. Ileana doesn't care about anyone as much as herself and the throne she clings to.

As the bullets fly and shouts echo around us, Damien and I find cover behind a grand statue. The marble image of a forgotten deity does little to calm the adrenaline coursing through my veins. I glance over at Damien, his eyes focused and calculating. He's assessing the situation, trying to find an opening, a chance for us to escape this madness.

"Just adapt the plan," Damien whispers, not taking his eyes off me. "You need to get her alone and kill her. That's the only objective."

I nod, swallowing hard. "It's going to be tough getting close to her. She suspects me because some bastard betrayed me."

"Work around it," he demands. I know my failure may mean the death of all of us. Failure isn't an option.

Gritting my teeth, I release a breath and make my move. Pushing off the statue, I plunge into the chaos, narrowly dodging the hail of bullets. My destination is the back rooms because I saw Ileana head that way. There are tunnels to escape, which is what she'll be attempting. My stomach drops when I enter the room where the tunnel entrance is. There's no sign of Ileana. A man I've never seen stands by the opening with a gun, guarding it. When he sees me, he smirks.

"There you are, Taren."

My brow furrows. "Who are you?"

"Santiago Castillo."

Hearing that name, it feels like all the blood in my body drains. Ileana told me all my family were dead, including my uncle.

The disbelief must be apparent on my face.

Santiago chuckles, a bitter sound echoing in the cold chamber. "Surprised to see me, nephew?" he taunts.

"I thought you were dead," I mutter, my heart pounding in my chest.

"Clearly, I'm not," he retorts, the smirk never leaving his face. His cold, dead eyes are devoid of any familial affection. "Ileana made a deal with me. My life for yours."

"But why?" I ask.

"Power, Taren. Pure and simple. I wanted to lead, and your father was in the way. So, I made a deal with the devil herself."

His confession sends a chill down my spine. This man, my own blood, sold my parents and sister out to the devil for power. And now, here he stands, a guard dog for the woman who destroyed our family.

"You had your own brother murdered?" I confirm.

He smirks. "I never liked your father. He got everything I didn't. The girl, the family." His jaw clenches. "Your mother should have been mine."

I glare at him, rage infecting my blood. I was sure Ileana was acting alone all this time, yet she had this bastard on the sidelines. The real reason my family died, even if he wasn't the one to kill them.

"It's a shame, really," Santiago continues, lifting his gun and pointing it directly at me. "You were always too weak. You could never handle the harsh realities of our world."

"I was eight years old, you fucking idiot." I tighten my grip around my own weapon. "What do you expect from a kid?"

"Your father and I were on the streets at that age."

I snort. "Yeah, and you were supposed to look out for each other. Instead, you had him murdered." I swallow the lump in my throat.

Santiago's finger moves to the trigger, and I realize that I've got two choices: kill or be killed. The choice becomes clear. I must survive. I must fight. I'm not the weak, naive boy Santiago perceives me to be. I'm stronger, and I'll prove it.

Before he can pull the trigger, I dodge to one side, my body reacting faster than my mind. My heart thunders in my chest as adrenaline courses through my veins, lending me the speed and precision I need. I aim, my hands steady while I focus on my target.

Santiago's arrogance gives me enough time to retaliate. My fingers squeeze the trigger, the gunshot reverberating in the cold entrance of the tunnel, and the bullet finds its mark.

Santiago's body crumples to the dusty ground, a

surprised expression etched on his face—my uncle, my betrayer, now lies lifeless with a bullet wound searing through his forehead.

It's often said, "Blood is thicker than water," implying family bonds are unbreakable. Yet, when family bonds turn treacherous, the bonds of blood can rupture, proving less resilient than friendships. In my world, the adage fails. And now it's time to kill the Red Queen and bathe in her blood, the way I watched her bathe in my family's blood.

29
ALICE

I'm frozen in fear where Ileana dropped me. My heart pounds in my ears as I watch bullets fly over my head. My mind is racing, trying to devise a plan to help, but I'm frozen like a deer in headlights.

Cowering like a fucking useless woman. I try to get my limbs to move, but they won't.

Suddenly Thiago's face appears above me. "Alice, we need to get you to safety."

I notice Matias by his side, and I never thought I'd be so relieved to see those two. They help me to my feet and then force me to sprint toward a huge column nearby. All three of us duck behind it as bullets ricochet off the stone, sending shards of it into the air.

I tense, glancing at Thiago who has never looked so on edge. "Where are we going?" I ask.

Thiago shakes his head. "We're getting you to safety. Taren's orders."

Matias growls. "Why would we want to save her when the image of her, bleeding and lifeless, seems so aesthetically pleasing?"

Thiago glares at him. "You know I often wonder why the fuck I haven't murdered you yet, as that would be rather aesthetically pleasing too."

Matias chuckles. "Because blood is thicker than water and all that."

I swallow hard as it's clear Matias isn't right in the head. He's not mad like Taren; he's psychotic, and I fear that somehow he's sunk his claws into Kali. Claws that we need to get out if we all make it out of here alive.

"Enough chit-chat. shouldn't we move?" I demand.

Thiago smirks. "I see why Taren like you, you're feisty." He glances around the column, looking for the perfect moment to move. "Okay, let's go fast and keep your head down."

He pushes away from the cover of the column and rushes toward the door Ileana dragged me through earlier. Trying to use me against Taren, unaware of his ultimate plan. That a rival cartel leader is in on it.

As the cacophonous chorus of machine guns resonates through the air, bullets zip by like lethal lightning. Each ricochet sends splinters of stone and debris flying like a grim fireworks display. We dart and weave, our every movement a gamble between life and death. With each shot, I flinch, my heart pounding in rhythm with the staccato of gunfire.

Thiago and Matias usher me through the door. I've never felt such poignant relief as the door slams shut behind us.

"Fuck me, that was intense," Thiago says, jaw clenched. "I'm going to need a bottle of tequila after this."

Matias shakes his head. "If we make it out alive."

"What now?" I ask.

They both look at me. "Now, we put you back in the holding room with Kali and Luna to make sure you're safe," Thiago says, grabbing my forearm.

"What about Taren?"

"Let us worry about him," Matias says.

I wouldn't trust Matias with Taren's life ever. He's too selfish and impulsive. They drag me into the holding room.

Luna jumps to her feet when she sees me rushing over. "Thank God you're okay!" She hugs me tightly, and I hug her back.

"Yeah, it's mayhem out there."

Kali approaches and hugs me, tears streaming down her face. "When we heard the commotion, we were sure you'd been killed."

I shake my head. "Takes more than a few bullets to kill me," I say, trying to remain upbeat despite the fact the entire plan has gone to shit.

Thiago clears his throat. "I need all three of you to remain here until we come get you. Got it?"

Luna looks ready to argue. And I want to argue, but I know they won't listen.

"It's too dangerous before you argue with me, bonita," Thiago says.

My brow furrows at the use of that nickname. A nickname that means beautiful in Spanish. Luna's shoulders drop, and she nods. "Okay." And then she steps toward him, reaching onto her tiptoes and kissing him softly.

Kali and I watch in surprise, mouths ajar.

"Please be careful," she whispers to him.

He cups her cheeks in his hands and gives her a tight smile. Just like Taren, he's unsure they can pull this off. "I'm always careful." He kisses her once more and then turns to his brother. "Let's go."

Matias clears his throat, eyes fixed on Kali. "Where's my kiss, little fairy?"

Kali glares at him. "I'd rather gouge my eyeballs out."

He chuckles, shaking his head. "Don't worry, that'll soon change."

Thiago grabs his brother's arm. "We need to get out there and end this."

Matias sobers and nods, holding his machine gun as they both disappear.

I turn to Luna and Kali. "I've got to find Taren."

Kali shakes her head. "You heard Thiago. It's too dangerous out there."

It doesn't matter what they say. Nothing is going to keep me in this cell. "I'm not sitting here doing nothing because if he..." I trail off, unable to say it as it scares me too much. Losing Taren would kill me.

"You going out there might distract him more, consider that," Luna advises.

She might be right, but I can handle myself. After what we've been through the last few weeks, it feels like I can handle anything as long as I'm by his side.

"There's no persuading me otherwise. I'll see you when this ends." I turn to leave.

"Alice," Luna says, stopping me and making me glance back at her. "Be careful."

I nod in response, and before they can say another word, I sprint out of the room and turn left. I heard

Ileana say she was going to the tunnels in the back room before she rushed away, leaving me in the chaos. And wherever she is, that's where Taren will be.

I run toward the back room and find the tunnel door open. When I see a body on the floor and blood beneath it, panic hits me. He's a similar size and build to Taren, but I feel relief when I see his face. It's not him.

I don't recognize him at all, but he has a bullet wound right through the center of his head. And his eyes are wide open. I expect to feel sickened by the sight of the blood and death, but I'm oddly unaffected. Ignoring my concern over my lack of reaction toward seeing a dead body so up close and personal, I walk past it and into the tunnel.

My footsteps echo off the walls as the tunnel grows darker and colder. The staccato of machine guns firing grows more and more distant as I push deeper into the darkness, away from the chaos but toward the storm. My breathing is the only sound punctuating the quietness.

And then I hear the distant drone of voices echoing ahead. My heart pounds so hard I can hardly hear anything else. This is it. There's no going back now. The man I inexplicably love is fighting his arch-nemesis, and I'll be by his side. If we don't make it out, then so be it. All I care about is being with him until the bitter end.

30

TAREN

I delve into the darkness of the tunnels, adrenaline pulsing through my veins and sharpening my senses.

Every sound, smell, and even my vision is heightened. The confrontation with my uncle has only inflamed my rage. And Ileana will meet my wrath. I'll bathe in her blood. I'll watch as the light slowly drains from her eyes and commit it to memory.

I sprint through the tunnels until I hear her voice echoing.

"Jorge, fucking keep up!" she demands.

I smirk. I hate Jorge, too, so I'll enjoy murdering him as well. The guy has been way too loyal to Ileana.

I move stealthily through the shadows, the silence of the tunnels working to my advantage. I inch closer, every step measured and soundless. When I'm within arm's length of Jorge, I strike. Using my left arm, I trap him in a chokehold, my right hand firmly pressing the cold steel of my knife against the soft flesh of his throat.

"Stop, Ileana," I command.

She spins around. The surprise in her eyes is rewarding, but the fear that follows is even more so. I've rarely seen fear in her eyes, but she's often inspired fear in my heart.

"Taren," she growls, eyes narrowing. "What the fuck do you think you're doing?"

I smirk. "I'm here to do what I should have done many years ago. Cut the head off the snake."

Her jaw clenches. "How did you get away from Damien?"

My smirk widens. "Haven't figured it out yet, Mother?" I tease, shaking my head. "Damien is here to help me get rid of you."

Her expression turns furious. "You traitorous son of a—"

"Shut up," I growl, feeling rage infiltrate every vein in my body. "Traitorous? How can I be fucking traitorous when I've no allegiance to you." I feel the heat of the rage overwhelm me. "You murdered my family in cold blood and made me watch as you filled a bathtub up with their blood and bathed in it."

The image flashes through my mind as I speak, threatening to break me apart. Images that have haunted me for twenty-two years. And then the images of her head severed from her body, but her eyes still open, flash through my mind. That's the goal. Keep a level head, Taren. You're so close.

"And then you made me call you Mother?" I snarl, nostrils flaring. "And I won't even mention the sick things you did to me or made me do, considering you made me call you that. Do you understand the sanctity of being a mother?" I spit, my anger bubbling over. "A mother is supposed to protect her child, love them, and teach them the world's ways. A mother should be the sanctuary in the chaos, a beacon of hope in despair. But you? You're the epitome of perversion. You've never been worthy of the title 'mother.' You never were my mother. My mother was murdered at your hands."

Ileana snarls at me. "I treated you better than that whore ever could."

I glare at her. "You didn't even know her."

She snorts. "How wrong you are, little boy."

"You knew my mother?" I confirm.

She nods. "Yes, and your father pretty well too."

Her jaw clenches. "I was in love with your father before he met your mother. And the bastard met her, and she stole him from me. It was only right once I became the queen of the Navarro cartel that I ended his sniveling excuse of a life. And I'm sure you met your uncle, Santiago."

"He's dead," I say, no emotion in my voice. "And you always were a sore loser. No wonder he didn't want to be with you. Who the fuck would?" I shake my head. "You've got no loyalty, and you're psychotic."

"Says the man who has the nickname the mad hatter and is currently betraying the woman who raised him."

"My riddles were all a rouse, you stupid bitch," I say, my blood boiling hotter. "If I was mad, it meant you couldn't see the true intent of my plans. The reason I stayed close despite wanting to murder you every single time I set eyes on you."

Ileana's attention moves behind me, and she smirks. "Alice, how good of you to join us."

I stiffen, wondering if she's playing games. However, the look in her eyes tells me she's not. It's pure delight. "Don't change the subject," I growl.

"Alice, why don't you come closer," Ileana says, ignoring me.

I glance briefly over my shoulder to find Alice

standing there like a fucking statue.

No.

Why did she come?

"Run back the way you came," I demand.

She looks at me defiantly and I know if we make it out of this alive, I'm going to give her a real punishment for this. Her actions might derail my entire plan. "No, I'm here to help."

Ileana laughs. "How can you help him? Pathetic little American girl captured on vacation." She sneers at her.

And then Alice pulls a gun, cocking it and aiming it right at Ileana. "I'll help him like this."

"I doubt you can even shoot that thing, why don't you—"

Alice shoots off a round above Ileana's head, cracking the tunnel roof slightly and showering her in dust. "My dad taught me how to shoot."

Ileana's face pales.

Jorge clears his throat. "Taren, I'm with you. Whatever you need, I'm on your side. She's got a grenade."

Ileana splutters, "You fucking traitorous piece of shit!"

"Toss all the weapons on your person over here," I say, ignoring Jorge's plea to switch sides. He knows he's on the losing side and wants to switch. It's the kind of man he is. And while I don't need him as such, if he does switch sides it will help with winning the rest of the cartel over. All of the men look up to him.

Ileana glares at Jorge as she tosses a gun and grenade over, the pin still in, luckily. While Ileana is insane, she's not crazy enough to blow herself up.

First, I need to test him. "Jorge, if you're serious about switching sides, then go and check her for weapons," I say, grabbing the gun Ileana tossed and aiming it at him. I glance at Alice. "You keep your gun on her. I'll cover Jorge."

Alice nods in response, and I've never been prouder of a person. In the eye of the storm, she's as calm as anything. My true equal. My true soul mate.

"Found this," Jorge says, grabbing a knife that was strapped to her calf.

I smirk as I had been aware she always keeps a knife there, and Jorge passed the test. "Good, chuck it to me."

Jorge chucks it over and then stands off to one side, giving Ileana a wide birth. "What can I help with?"

"Go back into the auction house and find Thiago and Damien; tell them I've got Ileana, and this will be over soon." I narrow my eyes. "All the men look up to you. Get them to stop fighting."

Jorge nods. "You've got it." He disappears the way Alice came, leaving the two of us with Ileana.

"Come now, Taren, surely we can talk—"

I fire my gun and hit the rock, too, showering her in more debris. "There's nothing to talk about. You're going to die today, Ileana. And it's about time."

The panic finally hits and she spins around, running in the opposite direction. I smirk, as the chase is part of the fun when it comes to hunting.

I chase after Ileana, Alice following close behind me. Ileana's desperation increases with each step, her breath ragged and echoing of the tunnel's walls. "You can't run forever. I'll catch you."

I savor the moment, letting adrenaline fuel me. This moment I've longed for since that day twenty-two years ago. I crouch down to pick up a rock and throw it, hitting Ileana's ankle and causing her to stumble and fall.

I approach and loom over her. "How shall I torture you first?" I ask, pulling my knife from my pocket again. "I want to hear you scream for a long time," I announce.

Alice stands a few feet away, and I glance at her. "You may not want to be here to see this, little bird."

She moves closer, shaking her head. "I don't only want to be here for this. I want to help. After hearing what she did to you. I want to burn her alive and record her screams and then listen to them on repeat."

Darkness. It lives in Alice like it lives in me. I believed she was pure light, but she's been touched by grief and trauma like me, and it's changed her. It may be why I've been drawn to her since we met.

"Okay, let's have some fun," I say, grinning as I grab Ileana and hoist her to her feet. "I know the perfect place."

"Taren, please—" I knock her over the head, making sure she's unconscious, and lift her over my shoulder.

"I'm not listening to her pleas any longer."

Alice nods. "Good, because if you hadn't knocked her out, I would have."

I laugh at her feistiness. It's a quality I admire.

My brow furrows. "You said your parents died when you were eight."

She nods in reply, her eyes full of sadness. "What's your point?"

"You said your dad taught you to shoot?"

"Yeah, my adoptive dad," she replies.

"Of course. Are you on good terms with your adoptive parents?"

I nod. "For the most part. They don't like that I chose to take creative writing at Brown, though."

I think on that as we start walking, every step echoing with the power of the moment. It's almost over.

"Where are you going to take her?" Alice asks.

I smirk. "Back to her house. It's only right this ends where it all started, right?"

She arches a brow. "If that were the case, you should take her to Mexico City."

It would be poetic to take her to the ruins in the city where she destroyed my life and turned my world upside down. But it's too risky. Mexico City wouldn't welcome Ileana with open arms, and having the officials take her from me would rob me of my retribution.

"True, but it's not that simple. The house will have to do."

Alice nods in response, stepping beside me as we exit the tunnels. A heavy silence falls between us as we make the short trek back to the house, the only sound of an owl hooting in the distance and the far-off rumble of cars on the road.

We head toward the end of an era. The Red Queen dies tonight, putting a stop to the vicious cycle of blood and fire she's showered me with since the day I met her.

31
ALICE

I watch Taren circle Ileana.

He brought her back to the house and tied her to her office chair. She's still out cold but has twitched and jolted a bit in the past minute, signaling she's coming back to consciousness.

"Are you sure you wish to be here for this?" he asks, not looking at me but keeping his eyes fixed on the woman who did unspeakable things to him.

I felt such anger when I heard Taren confronting her about what she did. I had a feeling she'd abused him physically, but hearing it... I want to kill her myself because, despite the crazy circumstances of how we met, I care about this man more than anyone on this earth.

He's complex and dark and broken but so beautiful. He could be more beautiful for it.

"I'm certain."

He keeps his gaze on Ileana. "It's going to get very bloody. I need to do what I want, and I can't have you going soft on me." Suddenly, Taren's gaze flicks to meet mine, his eyes dark and full of a strange vulnerability.

It's a look that slices through me, making my heart clench. "Get as bloody as you want. I won't get in your way, I promise."

"I'm going to bathe in her blood, literally," he says, as casually as if he told me he was going to order takeout. I wondered why he had the buckets.

A part of me isn't sure whether I can get on board with watching that, but I know I won't stop him. "If it gets too much, I'll simply leave. I won't stop you, I promise."

He nods, and as if on cue, Ileana begins to regain conciseness, groaning.

Her eyes flutter open, confusion etched onto her face at the sight of Taren and me. But beneath that confusion, I see the fear start to creep in. Good. She should be scared.

Taren was a vulnerable kid who had watched her murder his family and bathe in their blood. And then she took him, and I don't know the details, but it's clear she abused him. From what age, I can't be sure. All I know is I've never wanted some dead as badly as I want her dead. Not even Michael.

Taren steps forward, his footfalls echoing in the dimly lit room. "Are you ready to face the devil?" His voice is cold. "There's no way you're going anywhere but straight to hell. And if I'm heading there too, I don't care. It's worth it to watch you suffer a painful, horrific death."

Ileana struggles in her seat, the rope cutting into her wrists as she tries to get out of the seat. "Stop this madness, Taren!"

I step forward then, needing to question how she can call a man getting revenge for everything she's done mad. "The only mad one here is you. After what you did to Taren, how could you expect anything else?"

"Keep out of this gringo," she snaps, glaring at me.

Taren growls. "You don't speak to her like that." He moves forward and slaps her hard, the echo of skin against skin satisfying.

The look on Ileana's face is priceless. She's a woman who's never been put in her place.

"Taren, you don't want to do this, surely. I raised you." He ignores her and grabs a bucket, positioning it beneath her chair. And then he draws a knife from his pocket.

"I've got a rabbit to bleed." He smirks at her. "Didn't you wonder why I loved hunting and bleeding out animals? Because I was learning the best techniques to capture the most blood possible." He tilts his head. "There won't be enough to bathe, but I'll use your trick and half-fill it with water."

"W-what are you talking about?"

His smirk widens. "It'll be a fitting end for me to bathe in your blood after I'm done, won't it? The way I watched you bathe in my family's blood." He snarls, the rage spiking out of control. "After you made me carry the buckets to the bathtub."

Watching Taren, I struggle to understand how he's kept it together all these years. How he's managed to keep his rage at bay, waiting for the right moment. What she has done to him is unspeakable and unfathomable.

What monster makes a little kid do something like that?

Taren holds up the knife, and Ileana's eyes widen. She thrashes more violently, her desperate cries filling the air. But her struggle is futile.

He cuts her in methodical ways, the blood being

caught in the bucket perfectly. It's as if he's done this before.

Ileana's screams are piercing with each cut. The sight should make my stomach roll, but I'm surprisingly okay with it. The gore doesn't affect me how I'd expect.

As the bucket fills, I stand back and watch Taren. There's a satisfaction in his eyes, and I realize this is him finding his peace and freedom from a woman who has done nothing but take and abuse.

"How does it feel to be the one at the end of the blade, *Mother*?" he spits, using that word as a taunt.

Ileana's breathing is ragged, and her entire body is marred with deep cuts. Her eyes are dilated with pain so much they're just black now. "Taren, please—"

"I don't remember you listening to my family's pleas as they begged you to stop, including my four-year-old sister," he growls.

My stomach rolls again. Ileana did this to a little girl. I don't understand Taren and never will how he had the strength to remain under her oppression for so long, how he stopped himself from carrying this out for all that time until it was the right time.

Ileana's face is as pale as ash as she begins to shake from the blood loss.

Taren watches, his jaw clenched tight. "I want you to suffer as much as possible." He grabs her chin, forcing her to look at him. "Your pain is my fucking drug, and I'll drag this out as long as your body will take it, understand?"

Ileana doesn't respond, but there's resignation in her eyes. She knows there's no stopping this.

He continues his torture, cutting and slicing until she's struggling to draw breath and is on the brink of death. The bucket is almost full. I don't see how it's enough to bathe in, though.

Her breathing becomes rattly as she lingers between the veil. Death is merely moments away, and that's when Taren stops. "You will die soon, but I won't take away your pain. I won't plunge this knife into your heart. I want you to suffer." He discards the knife on the floor and steps back, staring at her with a hatred so dark I'm surprised it hasn't consumed him.

We stand in silence; the only sound is the rattle of her breath until finally, she takes one last gasping inhale before falling silent. Her eyes are still open but glassy and vacant.

Taren cracks his neck and exhales deeply. "Freedom," he murmurs.

I grind my teeth, wondering whether he truly feels free. Surely, all the trauma this woman put him through can't even begin to be erased by this.

"Let's go, little bird," he says, grabbing the bucket beneath her chair. "I need a bath."

I follow him up the stairs to his bathroom, where he turns on the faucet and waits for the bath to fill halfway. And then he adds the blood.

Taren slides into the macabre bath. The crimson liquid has dyed the clear water. He sighs with contentment and rests his head back, eyes closed as if he's in a normal bathtub filled with lavender-scented bubbles instead of the symbol of his vengeance.

I stand at the doorway, the metallic scent of blood heavy in the air. I can't tear my gaze away from the scene. The water is now a deep, murky red. Taren looks more like a creature from a nightmare than a man. His satisfaction is palpable, making the scene even more horrifying. And yet, I understand it. She did this to his family, and he feels the need to do it to her.

I watch Taren, his face partially masked by the steam rising from the tub, an eerie calmness exuding from him. It's a chilling sight that will haunt me in my dreams, a stark reminder of the darkness we're all capable of. A reminder that the man I love is twisted beyond imagination.

"The Red Queen is dead," he mutters, eyes still shut. "I've never felt lighter."

After about ten minutes, he finally opens his eyes and they meet mine instantly. "Turn on the shower." He tilts his head. "I need to wash her off me."

I walk toward the shower, turning on the faucet.

"Strip too," he demands, his voice hard and unwavering.

I glance back at him as he stands in the bath, the bloody water clinging to his tanned skin. He looks like something from a horror film, yet I don't feel horror. I'm more horrified that I'm turned on right now. And then I notice his cock is hard.

I strip off my clothes as instructed.

"Get in," he instructs.

I step under the warm, soothing spray of the water, watching as he makes his way from the bath to the shower, bloody water dripping from him onto the cream tiles.

I can't take my eyes off him. My heart pounds so hard I can't hear anything above the blood rushing in my ears.

As Taren steps into the shower, the blood from his body swirls down the drain, replaced with clean water. He looks at me, and the distance between us vanishes in a heartbeat. We come together in a passionate and vicious clash, our bodies meeting in a collision of raw desire and unspoken need.

Our lips meet in a ferocious kiss, fierce and demanding. When Taren breaks free for air, he whispers against my lips. "I've never felt more free. Perhaps we're both birds now." He lifts me off the floor, forcing me to wrap my legs around his muscled hips. And then he slams my back into the wall, his hard cock resting against my entrance. "I need you," he breathes.

I moan, digging my nails into his skin as the need to have him inside me is all-consuming. A deep ache spreads through my center.

"Fight me," he breathes. "I like it when we play."

I swallow hard, my pussy getting wetter. Why do I love it so much when we role-play rape fantasy? I'll never understand it, but I think it's time I stop trying to understand the complexities of our relationship and embrace the darkness. It's a part of both of us.

"Stop this," I say, beating my fists against his chest.

He bites my neck hard enough to make me squeal. "Never. You belong to me." His cock rubs against my clit, teasing me as I bite my lip to stop myself from moaning.

"I don't want this. Don't you know the meaning of stop?" I dig my nails into his skin and scrape them down his chest, making him hiss.

"You're just making me harder," he growls, and then, with one vicious slam of his hips, his cock slides inside me. "So fucking wet for a dirty little bird who says she doesn't want this."

I growl and glare at him. "Stop this right now!"

He smirks in response. "Make me."

It's a challenge, and I realize he wants me to fight harder, so I do. I claw my fingers into his scalp, pulling him toward me and biting his lip.

He growls into my mouth. "Naughty, Alice." He pulls out of me and then forces me to turn around, pressing my body against the glass of the shower. "You made me bleed."

"Good," I spit back.

And then he slams into me with such force he steals the breath from my lungs. His hips piston harder and faster as he fucks me against the glass. And I've never been more turned on as his aggression increases.

I love surrendering my control to him. The darkness eating at me for years, particularly the last two years, eases when we're together. It doesn't make sense, but his darkness is a balm for mine.

"My beautiful, filthy bird," Taren growls darkly in my ear. "You get off on this, don't you? Being used, being raped like this?" His thrusts turn bruising, each one a potent reminder of his dominance and my submission.

His teeth graze my earlobe as he hisses, "It's twisted. How you crave my darkness, how you find solace in this fucked-up dance we're entwined in." Our darkness is interlinked, a perverse symbiosis neither of us can fully comprehend.

"No, you bastard. Stop!" I maintain my role in our perverse play.

He chuckles. "And yet your cunt is clinging to me as if it never wants me to leave. You're going to come, aren't you?"

I shake my head, but it's a lie. I'm so close to exploding and shattering it's shameful.

"Don't lie to me," he growls. His grip on my hip tightens, anchoring me against the chilling glass as he continues his relentless assault.

"Let go, Alice," he commands, his voice holding that edge of darkness I've grown to crave. "Show me how much you love me owning you."

The coil in my belly tightens, my body responding to his commands. With a cry, I surrender to the wave of pleasure, my body clenching around him as my orgasm tears through me, his name a hoarse shout on my lips.

"Good girl," Taren murmurs into my ear, his thrusts slowing. "Now I'm going to fill you with my cum," he announces, slamming into me harder and spiking the pleasure higher. After a few more vicious thrusts, he buries himself deep and explodes, his cock twitching inside me as he sinks his teeth into my shoulder.

When he's finished, he pulls out of me and spins me around, pulling me into his chest. I curl tight to him, feeling at home in his arms. His darkness may be a balm for mine, but his tenderness is what truly heals me. I want to be lost in our world where dysfunction makes sense forever.

ALICE

The soft hum of the jet engines is all that sounds as I sit by Taren's side, my stomach a mess. What we just went through. All the emotions I witnessed the man before me go through as he cut down his oppressor will stay with me for a long time.

"Where are we going?" I ask softly.

Taren turns to me, his face a mask of composed tranquility. "We're heading to the airport," he answers, his gaze resolute. "Boston awaits."

"Boston?" I ask.

He nods. "I've got a professor to torture."

My heart skips a beat. Taren remembered.

Luna and Kali look confused. "A professor?" Luna asks.

"Professor Lovell."

Kali shakes her head. "What? Why would you kill Alice's English professor."

Taren turns to look at me. "You haven't told them?"

I bite the inside of my cheek, shaking my head.

"I apologize for speaking out of turn, little bird."

I sigh heavily. "It's fine." I glance at my friends, who look confused. "Two years ago, Professor Lovell raped me," I admit.

The following silence is deafening, only broken by the soft hum of the jet's engines. Luna and Kali stare at me, their faces a mixture of shock and confusion. Finally, Luna breaks the silence. "Why the hell didn't you tell us?" she demands, her voice choked.

I glance at her, my heart aching at her teary eyes. "I don't know," I confess, my voice quiet. "I was scared and ashamed."

Luna moves closer, wrapping an arm around my shoulders. "You should never be ashamed of anything around us. We're your best friends."

Kali nods. "You should have told us. And to think, we gave you all that shit about dating..."

I swallow hard, tears prickling my eyes. "I know. I'm sorry I didn't say anything. I wanted to forget about it..."

Taren growls. "Well, that bastard Michael probably

did, too, but he won't touch another woman again. Not once, I'm through with him."

Luna's brow furrows. "You're going to kill him?"

Taren's attention moves to her. "It's best not to ask questions you don't want the answer to."

We all know that means yes. And while both my friends look horrified, I'm ashamed to admit I'm thankful. I want him dead for the trust that he broke because, deep down, I'm as dark as Taren. And I'm not sure I want to admit that to my friends. It's crazy that despite knowing them far longer than Taren, I feel more comfortable bearing my soul to him than anyone.

Kali sighs. "He deserves whatever's coming to him. A professor is supposed to be someone you can trust. If he's done it to Alice, God knows how many other girls he's violated."

As the conversation lulls, I glance out of the aircraft's window, Mexico shrinking as we climb higher into the sky. The silence in the cabin echoes my inner turmoil. The revelation has taken a toll on us all.

"What about Blake?" I say, shaking my head. "We should be rescuing her first. She's more important."

Taren's jaw clenches. "That's a more delicate task. The man she was sold to is one of the most powerful men in Mexico. Certainly the richest."

My stomach churns. "Then we should be heading to wherever Gaston is and save Blake. We shouldn't be going to Boston."

Taren's eyes meet mine, carrying a sincerity that sends a shiver down my spine. "We will, Alice, I promise. But first, there's some important business I need to deal with in Boston, not just Michael." It looks like a heavy weight is on his shoulders. "I must secure my position as leader of the Navarro Cartel. And our stateside operations are stationed in Boston."

I bite the inside of my cheek as I wonder what that means for us. How do we have a future? A Brown university student and a cartel leader.

"Why are Matias and Thiago coming?" I ask, noticing they both disappeared through a door to the back of the plane when we got on.

"Because they're the only two I trust to station in the stateside operation and report back to me."

"So you'll be living in Mexico?" I confirm.

A flash of something passes through his eyes. "Yes, we will be."

I shake my head. "I've got to finish my senior year at Brown."

Darkness crosses his eyes. "I can't be away from you, baby."

I swallow hard. "I've worked hard on this degree. I really want to finish it."

He nods. "Fine, I'll be with you until you finish."

"What about the Cartel?" I ask.

"I'll have to go back and forth. It's not ideal, but I'll make it work." He squeezes my hand. "For you, I'll make anything work."

Something heavy squeezes around my heart. Hearing Taren say that makes me feel so many emotions. I've always buried my emotions for as long as I can remember. When my parents and sister died, it was as if I died with them. A part of me missing from day-to-day life. I can't believe how many similarities I share with this man.

Thiago and Matias reappear from the back in fresh clothes free of blood. "The bedroom is all yours," Thiago announces, smirking at Taren. "You need to clean up before we get to Boston."

Taren's jaw clenches. "We both do." He squeezes my thigh. "And after, Kali and Luna can get clean and dressed."

I grind my teeth, unsure about leaving my two friends with those monsters. Luna may have feelings for Thiago for some fucked up reason, but Kali is vulnerable, and Matias is a fucking wolf preying on a lamb.

"Are you two going to be okay?" I ask, glancing at the two men staring at my friends as if they're meat on a plate.

"Yes, we'll be fine," Luna replies.

Taren gives Thiago and Matias warning glares. "Behave."

And then he leads me into the back, where there's a bedroom and adjoining bathroom.

"Sit down," he says, nodding at the bed. He pulls his bloodied shirt off and discards it to one side.

I sit and stare up at him. "Are we going to shower?"

He nods. "In a moment. I need to know you're okay."

"Why wouldn't I be?"

His eyebrows raise. "After what you saw me do to—"

"I relished it, Taren. I thought that was clear. She deserved everything she got and more."

He smiles. "Perfect little bird." He cups my cheeks and sits by my side. "How are you so dark?"

"Life," I murmur, shrugging.

"Your family's death wasn't your fault," he says.

I clench my jaw. "They were on the way to collect me. They died, and I survived. It's natural to feel guilty."

He nods. "It is. I can't tell you how often I wished

Ileana had murdered me with my parents and sister. At least then I wouldn't have to live with the images of them being tortured, maimed, and then burned."

I glance at his stomach. "Did Ileana burn you?"

He grinds his teeth and shakes his head. "I went through a stage of self-harm."

I draw in a deep breath as the burn marks are all over his stomach. He must have hurt himself a lot. "Oh."

"I'm broken, little bird. Are you sure you want all my rough pieces?"

I look at Taren, really look at him. His body is a map of scars and burns, but his eyes bear the deepest wounds. "I'm not afraid of your rough pieces, Taren," I whisper. "I've got my own." I reach out, tracing the burns on his stomach with my fingers. "We're both broken. Maybe together, we're whole."

He kisses me then.

Taren's eyes darken as he softly lifts my hand from his scars and kisses my knuckles. "I'm going to fuck you," he announces.

"But what—"

He silences me with a hand against my mouth. "And I don't want to hear another word from your mouth." He's forceful as he grabs me and tosses me onto my back on the bed, looming over me.

"Strip."

I do as he says, quickly shedding my clothes under his intense gaze. The air between us is electric, and the room is filled with anticipation. He watches me. "Now, let me see you," he instructs, his voice rough with desire. "Play with yourself for me like you did before."

My heart pounds hard in my chest as he watches me expectantly. Slowly, I slide my fingers to my center, circling my clit with them and moaning. "Fuck," I murmur, finding I'm so sensitive. I always am around this God of a man.

"That's it, baby. Let me see you play with yourself. Are you thinking about me raping you?"

I meet his gaze and nod, biting my bottom lip. "Yes."

"Dirty little Alice." He unzips his pants and pulls his cock out, stroking it.

Taren's dark gaze intensifies, his hand moving faster up and down his thick length. "You like being taken? The idea of me using you?" He asks.

"Yes," I gasp, my fingers working in rhythm with his strokes. The heat in the room becomes a tangible entity, wrapping us in its fiery grasp.

"That's it, baby," he gets onto the bed and crawls toward me. His free hand brushes softly up my inner thigh. His touch is like a live wire, sending shockwaves of pleasure through my body.

Taren's gaze never leaves mine, the intensity of it pushing me to the brink. "You're so beautiful like this," he breathes out. "So open, so ready. You are ready for me, aren't you?"

"Yes," I whimper, my body trembling under the weight of his gaze.

Taren flashes a dark and predatory grin. "Good girl," he murmurs, leaning close. "I'm going to make you scream. Everyone on this plane will hear what I'm doing to you," he growls.

I should feel mortified at the idea of my friends hearing us, but it only turns me on more.

What has this man done to me?

Taren wastes no time. In a swift motion, he enters me, filling me to the hilt. His groan of pleasure echoes in the small bedroom, mingling with my gasp.

The world narrows to the feel of him inside me, powerful and insistent. As he moves, each thrust is a perfectly timed symphony that pushes me toward the edge faster than I've ever known. "You like that, baby?" he breathes out, his voice a low rumble of pure sin. "You like feeling me inside you?"

His dirty talk fuels the fire, ramping up the intensity of my arousal. Each time with him is so raw and passionate that I'm shocked. The way he touches me, the way he looks at me, I'm addicted.

"So tight, so wet," he growls, driving into me harder, faster. The pleasure is overwhelming. It's all I can do to hang on, to ride the wave of pleasure he's eliciting within me.

"Taren," I moan. "I'm going to—"

He grabs my throat and blocks my airway. "No, not until I give you permission."

Taren continues to move, his rhythm unyielding and his control absolute. His thumb of his free hand swipes over my lips, and his eyes lock onto mine. "You're mine, do you understand?" He grinds out, each word punctuated by a thrust that steals my breath.

"Yes," I manage to breathe, the room spinning as his pace quickens.

Taren's grip on my throat loosens enough for me to gather a lungful of air, but the dominance in his eyes never fades. He's a man in full control, and I'm utterly his.

Suddenly, he slows, his strokes becoming deliberate and tortuously slow.

I'm on edge, desperate, needing release. "Please..." I sob out, but he shakes his head.

"Not yet, baby," he murmurs, a smirk on his lips. "You come when I say so."

And with that, he plunges deep within me again, setting a maddening pace that has my world tilting on its axis. I cling to him, lost in the man who's taken me beyond the realms of pleasure and into something far more dangerous: complete surrender.

And I wouldn't have it any other way. His presence is like a potent drug coursing through my veins, making me crave him more. We're playing a dangerous game, and yet, I can't seem to pull away. I'm lost in him, intoxicated by this perilous love, and I don't want to be found.

33

TAREN

I circle the pathetic excuse of a man before me.

The mere thought of him putting his hands on my little bird turns me savage. The knife in my jacket pocket is burning a hole through the fabric. All I want is to watch him bleed and delight in his screams.

They say madness breeds madness.

There's no removing the dark, twisted part of me that Ileana forged. It's too deeply embedded in who I am, and I'll embrace it. There's no point running from yourself.

"He's waking up." Alice's voice pulls me from my thoughts as I notice Michael is starting to stir.

I arch a brow. "Are you ready to be free?"

Alice's eyes meet mine, glinting with anticipation.

"Yes," she says, her voice steady. "I've been waiting for this for two years."

I nod, my gaze never leaving the man who dared to harm her. He grunts as he wakes up, and then panic sets in. "What the fuck? Where am I?" He's got a hood over his head, so he's woken in darkness

"You're at your reckoning, Michael."

He stiffens at the sound of my voice. "Who are you? What do you want?"

I smirk at the hint of fear in his voice. I'm going to enjoy this. Especially knowing how much he fucked with my little bird's head. "To bathe in your blood."

He trembles. "Please. I don't know who you are or what you want, but I've got money. I can pay—"

"Your money doesn't mean anything to me. All I want is your pain and fear to pay for what you did."

Alice steps forward, her face a mask of steely determination. "You took something from me, Michael," she says, her voice eerily calm. "You violated my sense of safety, peace, and trust." She pauses, her gaze never leaving the trembling man before her. "Now, it's time you learn what it's like to have something taken from you."

Michael starts to whimper, recognizing her voice. "Alice? Are you insane?"

She laughs bitterly. "Insane? I've never been more sane in my life."

I've never felt more connected to someone in my life. As I stare at her, I know my instincts are right. She's destined to be my queen.

"Take off the hood, baby. Look the monster in the eye. Show him the fear he instilled in you has morphed into power," I tell her.

She takes off the hood, revealing his terrified face. "Are you scared?" she asks, looking at him.

His lip trembles.

"You know, I was scared too when you pushed me onto the ground after I'd told you no three times." She tilts her head. "I was scared when you pushed up my skirt and ripped down my panties and then shoved yourself inside me as I screamed for you to stop." Her jaw clenches. "And I was so fucking scared, I didn't even tell one after it happened." She glances at me. "Until I met my soulmate."

"You've lost the plot, Alice. You'll end up in prison for this."

I laugh, then. "Not if no one ever finds the body. And believe me, no one ever will."

Michael turns the shade of ash as he starts to sob.

Pathetic.

"How shall we start?" I ask, knowing she wants to

lead on this. And despite trying to persuade her it was a bad idea to be present, I can't deny Alice this chance. It would be like someone denying my revenge on Ileana, and whoever said revenge doesn't make you feel better was lying. I've never felt more free.

"I want to watch him suffer." She looks at me. "Whatever way will hurt the most."

How she's grown. The little timid, broken bird I met in that basement has evolved into a fierce and beautiful eagle, and she's soaring high.

"Believe me, I know hundreds of ways to make him hurt. And I'll use everyone until he dies from shock."

Michael quivers. "Come on, you're not a killer, Alice."

Alice glares at him. "I wasn't, but you've turned me into someone I hardly recognize anymore." She gets closer to him. "How many girls are there like me that you've violated?"

He shakes his head. "I don't know what you're talking about."

"A cowardly liar to the bitter end, then?" I ask.

"Who the fuck are you?" Michael asks.

I tilt my head, and a grin spreads across my face. "People often call me the Mad Hatter, Michael," I admit. "A fitting nickname for someone who delights in torture, don't you think?" I circle him slowly, my footsteps echoing on the concrete. "However, who I am is the boss of one of the most powerful cartels in Mexico."

The revelation lands with the weight of a thousand bricks, and Michael's fear-soaked face tells me he understands the grave reality of his situation. I know what I'm doing. My life revolves around crime, and I'll make him disappear without a trace.

"Please, don't do this," Michael begs. His eyes, wide with terror, dart between Alice and me. "I can pay you. I've got powerful connections. This doesn't have to end this way."

Alice laughs. "We told you we don't need your money, only your pain."

I pull out my knife, the cool steel gleaming under the harsh fluorescent lights.

Michael's breath hitches, and then the coward pisses himself. A dark patch stains his pants.

I frown. "Are you a man or a mouse, Michael? As I'm thinking, it's the latter. Face the consequences of your actions with more dignity. After all, God is watching."

I walk over to Michael, my fingers lightly dancing along the knife's edge. Plunging the blade into his thigh, I revel in the howl of pain that echoes through the warehouse.

No one hurts my little bird and gets away with it. Not while there's a beat in my heart or oxygen in my lungs. I will burn this world until it's just the two of us if that's what it takes to keep her safe and protected.

Michael writhes, his screams turning into desperate pleas for mercy. But mercy has no place here, not tonight.

Alice steps forward. Her eyes glitter with an insatiable thirst for revenge. She grabs a rusted iron rod from the corner of the room and, without hesitation, strikes Michael's knee with all her strength. A sickening crunch fills the air, accompanied by another gut-wrenching scream.

A wicked smile creeps onto Alice's face, a face that I once deemed as innocent. But there's nothing innocent about my sadistic little bird. Her wings are broken and battered like mine, and I wouldn't have it any other way.

"Was it worth it now, Michael?" she taunts, her voice filled with a cruel delight. "Worth the five minutes of rape to feel this kind of pain. How many came before and after me? Answer that, at least."

Michael can't even stop screaming, let alone answer a question. I don't think she'll get her answer.

We continue in the same fashion, cutting and beating him until he's on the edge of death. He coughs, making a gurgling sound as the blood pools in the back of his throat. His eyes, now void of the arrogance they once held, are filled with terror as he gazes at Alice and me.

Alice walks toward me, her blood-stained hands reaching for me. She looks at me with those hypnotic eyes, the burning hatred in them having cooled down to a content satisfaction.

"Shall we end this?" she inquires, her voice barely above a whisper.

I nod, my grip tightening on the knife. The end is near for Michael. And with his end, a new chapter is set to begin for Alice and me. A chapter penned with blood and revenge, bound by our twisted love.

With that, we move in unison, the rusted iron rod and the knife finding their last mark on Michael's body. His final scream echoes through the warehouse before everything falls silent. An eerie calm descends upon us, the only sound being the harsh intake and release of our ragged breaths.

As Michael's lifeless body slumps forward, Alice and I turn toward each other. Our clothes are splattered with blood, our hands trembling with the adrenaline that courses through our veins.

Alice is my queen, and she'll be perfect and strong by my side. Without a word, I pull her toward me, our bodies colliding with a force that echoes our raw, primal emotions. The table nearby becomes our altar as we surrender ourselves to our carnal desires, the taste of revenge still lingering on our tongues.

"Fuck me," Alice growls.

I make quick work of removing her panties and unzip my pants before slamming into her with force.

Her back arches, and her nipples are hard and pointed through the thin fabric of her dress. A beautiful moan tumbles from her lips.

I've got no control anymore as I slide in and out of her tight cunt. The wet sounds, coupled with her skin slapping together, make a perverse symphony. If anyone could see this sight, they'd be shocked.

I get the rapist's blood on her clothes, and she gets it on mine, but neither of us cares. We're free. We're flying high. And our love is the only thing that matters.

Every moan from her lips, and the more she arches toward me, the harder I fuck her. Alice loves it hard and rough.

"That's it, baby. Take every inch in that cunt. I love how turned on you get after getting revenge on people," I murmur into her ear.

She moans and claws her fingers down my chest. "I love watching you in action."

I kiss her, swallowing her moans as the words I want to say are on the tip of my tongue. I fucking love her. I knew I did the moment I set eyes on her.

My hands find their way to her waist, gripping the soft flesh as I continue to move within her. The blood on our bodies is now a shared mark, a testament to the journey we've embarked on together. I can feel her walls clenching around me, her body trembling with the impending climax. But I want this moment to last, to live in the stark reality of our shared darkness.

"Slow down, Alice," I breathe, my voice barely a whisper. "Only come when I tell you to."

Her eyes lock with mine, and she bites her lip. "But I'm so close."

"Be a good girl for me," I coax, my thumb rubbing circles on her clit. "Wait for me."

My words cause her to cling tighter, her nails digging into my skin. Her breath comes out in short, ragged gasps, her eyes filled with wild, untamed lust.

My control slips, and the pace quickens again, each thrust bringing us closer to the edge.

"Please, Taren," she begs, her voice hoarse. "I need to... I can't..."

"What is it, baby?" I tease, knowing she's on the edge and desperate for release.

"Please let me come," she demands, her sky-blue eyes so dilated.

I chuckle at her desperation, my pleasure heightened by the power I hold over her. "Begging?" I taunt. The friction between us continues to build, her body squirming beneath me in anticipation. "Remember, Alice, patience is a virtue."

She whimpers in response, her fingers digging into my skin in her struggle for control. "Taren, please..."

I kiss her neck, my hot breath fanning against her soft skin. "Keep begging, little bird," I purr, relishing the sweet torture. "I love hearing your pleas."

As her cries reach a fever pitch, I lean in and whisper against her ear, "Come for me, Alice. Show me how good it feels to be owned by me."

"Fuck," she cries, shaking her head. "It feels like heaven." Her body trembles, and her cunt tightens around me, pulling me right over the edge with her.

I sink my teeth into her neck, biting her as my cock explodes and I spill my cum deep inside her. I claw at her hips, making sure I leave bruises. Marks of my ownership of her. "Such a good girl taking all of my cum like that," I murmur into her ear, still moving my hips and not wanting this moment to end.

"Taren?" she says my name and her voice is vulnerable.

"Yes?" I pull back to look into her eyes, knowing I've never seen anyone look at me the way she is.

"I love you," she whispers.

I tense initially, those three words so foreign to my ears. And yet, I know I feel the same. I knew the moment I saw my little bird in her cage that I loved her and always will.

"You don't have to—"

I kiss her before she can say another word, my tongue delving deep into her mouth. And when we're both breathless, I brush a loose strand of hair from her face, my fingers trailing down her cheek. "In the depths of your eyes, I've found a home more comforting than any I've known. In the rise and fall of your breath, I've discovered a symphony that soothes my restless heart. I love you, Alice, for who you are and the man I become with you. You're my salvation, my purpose, my little bird."

But as the afterglow fades, I can't help but notice the stark contrast of our surroundings to the feelings flooding me.

The sight of Michael's lifeless body serves as a chilling reminder of the darkness inside us. Darkness that drives us and bonds us.

I shift my gaze back to Alice to find her also

looking at Michael, an unreadable look in her eyes. "Are we monsters?" she asks.

"Our oppressors were monsters, and we've cut them down. We're monster slayers, and I will slay any monster that tries to hurt you."

Her lips press together, and she doesn't say anything; she moves closer to me and rests her head on my chest. At that moment, I know that there is nothing I wouldn't do for this woman.

There's comfort in our silence, a sort of unspoken communication that echoes warmly within the vast emptiness.

We've become architects of our morality, justifying the blood on our hands as necessary for our freedom. It's our world, which we've fashioned from the ashes of our pasts. We live in this paradox, this captivating nightmare, and somehow, it feels like home.

I stare at the skyscraper Gaston Marques calls home, then turn to Alice. "You need to stay somewhere safe." I nod to the cafe fifty yards from us. "In there."

Alice stares at me defiantly. "No chance. I'm going in with you. Blake is my friend."

I sigh, knowing better than to argue with her in this state. "Fine, but stay close." We push through the revolving doors, our hearts pounding in sync with the echo of our footsteps against the marble floor.

The security guard steps forward the moment he sees me. "You don't live here. State your business."

I steel my gaze, knowing this is going to be nearly impossible. The Elysium is the most secure building in

Mexico City. It's nearly impenetrable. I can only rely on his Gaston being stupid enough to give me access. "I'm here for a meeting with Gaston Marques."

The guard's eyes narrow. "There's no meeting on the calendar."

"Call him and ask him," I suggest.

"If you're fucking with me, I'll kill you. Gaston hates being interrupted," the guard warns.

My heart pounds erratically as he calls his apartment.

"What is it?" Gaston snaps.

"A man is here saying he has a meeting with you. Is that true?"

"What's his name?"

"Taren," I say.

There are a few moments of silence before Gaston speaks, "Send him up."

"He's with a girl," the guard adds, looking Alice up and down in a way that makes me want to choke the life out of him. I would if we weren't on a mission to save her friend.

Gaston chuckles. "Send them both up."

A look of surprise crosses the guard's face, but he steps aside and allows us to cross to the private elevators. We step into the polished cabin, and I press the button for the penthouse. As the elevator ascends, I turn to Alice, her face pale in the artificial light. "Remember, stick to the plan. In and out, that's it."

She nods, her grip tightening on my arm.

The doors slide open to reveal Gaston lounging in a lavish living room, a smug smile on his face.

Blake is dressed in a stunning gown that must have cost a fortune. Her eyes widen when she sees Alice. "Alice! What are you doing here?"

Gaston glares at her. "Quiet, beautiful."

Her jaw clenches, and she falls silent.

"They're here to save you, aren't you?" Gaston asks, looking between me and Alice.

I walk into the room, approaching him with Alice by my side. "Is there anything I can give you to consider parting with your purchase?" I ask, knowing that Gaston is a powerful man. Taking her against his will is like painting a target on your back.

He rubs his jaw. "What do you think, beautiful?" he asks, looking at Blake. "Do you want to leave?"

I notice the obvious flash of indecision in Blake's eyes. She's been here for weeks, beaten down and broken. She should be jumping at the idea.

And then she turns to Gaston. She says something, but it's too quiet for us to hear. He leans toward her and whispers in her ear. And then, when he pulls back, I'm surprised to see the anguish in his eyes.

Gaston straightens, still holding Blake's gaze. There's a brief silence before he finally says, "You can go, beautiful." His voice is rough and strained.

It's not the response I was expecting. I study Gaston, noticing how his eyes never leave Blake and the raw pain he's poorly concealing.

Against all odds, Gaston cares for her. Really cares for her beyond the possessive obsession I noticed in the basement when he saw her. He wants her. She's more to him than an object, a possession to be flaunted. Yet, he's letting her go. Letting her walk away from him despite everything.

Blake gives him one last glance, a frown marring her beautiful features before she approaches us.

Blake pauses momentarily, glancing at Gaston over her shoulder. Something unspoken passes between them, a silent, final goodbye. "Thank you for letting me go," she murmurs, her voice barely audible.

Her tone is clear, full of quiet gratitude and an undercurrent of sorrow. This moment, this act of mercy from the man who had been her captor, marks the end of a chapter in her life. It's an admission that despite the circumstances, Gaston had grown to care for her in his own complex way, and she for him.

Once inside the sanctuary of the elevator, with the metal doors firmly shut behind us, Blake finally breaks. A tremor runs through her, and then she's crying. The sobs make her body tremble while her tears fall like rain down her sun-kissed cheeks. Alice immediately pulls her into a warm, comforting embrace, holding her firmly as she crumbles in her arms. The silent strength of Alice's support is apparent, and she has become an anchor for Blake in this turbulent storm.

I stand there, somewhat shocked. I hadn't expected that rescue to be so easy or that Gaston would just let her go. When we get to the ground floor of Elysium, we walk onto the sidewalk, only to be stopped by a chauffeur. "Mr. Marques has arranged for me to take you to the airport."

I narrow my eyes. "Why?"

His jaw clenches. "Mr. Marques doesn't explain himself to me."

"Because I'm coming with you," a deep, velvet voice speaks behind me.

I turn around to find Gaston standing with baggage in his hands. "What the fuck?"

Blake steps forward. "What do you mean you're coming? I thought you said—"

"I'll win you over back in your country. Where you

feel most comfortable." There's a dark flicker in his eyes. "I love a challenge, as you know, bella." He tilts his head. "Not to mention, you look pretty torn over parting with me anyway."

Alice shakes her head. "She's upset because of the trauma you put her through!"

Gaston ignores her. "Is that what she said?"

"She doesn't need to," Alice says.

I draw in a deep breath. "You coming wasn't the deal."

Gaston smirks. "I didn't make any deal. I merely said Blake is free to go, and she is, but I'm going too."

Blake growls. "You're unbelievable."

His smirk only widens. "I know." And then he gets into the back of the limo, looking at us expectantly.

Alice shakes her head. "Can't we ignore him and go in our taxi?"

Gaston clears his throat. "Do it. I dare you. See what happens."

I growl. "You better not be threatening my girl."

His smirk grows. "I knew you had a thing for the gringo when I was looking at them. I must admit, it tempted me to mess with you." He shrugs. "But I couldn't resist my beautiful angel."

Blake flushes a little at the use of that nickname.

"Get in," he demands.

We all exchange glances before reluctantly getting into the car with him. He's powerful. And not in the way that Ileana was powerful. Gaston could have any of us disappear without a trace, and no one could link it back to him.

Blake tries to sit opposite Gaston, but he grabs her wrist and forces her next to him. He firmly grips her thigh. "Don't worry, beautiful. I had no intention of really letting you go. You're too damn addictive."

"And you're a cocky asshole," she retorts.

He isn't angry; he merely ignores her. "A cocky asshole who owns you."

Alice sits by my side, her brow furrowed as she watches her friend with the man who bought her. And silence falls over the back of the limo, cloaked in tension. Gaston's grip tightens on Blake's thigh. She swallows down her fear, her gaze never leaving his. "I don't belong to anyone," she insists.

He chuckles, his pale blue eyes gleaming under the dim light. "We shall see, beautiful."

Alice and I share a glance. This isn't over. Our rescue mission remains incomplete as long as Gaston possesses this unsettling power over Blake.

I wrap an arm around Alice, hoping to offer

comfort. I can feel her worry mirroring my own. The rest of the ride is silent, each of us lost in our thoughts. Only time will tell whether Blake can break free of this powerful man's shackles, but something tells me it's her fight. And none of us can fight it for her.

EPILOGUE

ALICE

One year later…

Under a sky streaked with hues of a setting sun and serenaded by the soothing whispers of the ocean, I watch Blake as she moves down the aisle marked out on the sand. This place is beautiful and must have cost a fortune, not that cost matters to her husband.

She looks like a golden-haired angel, eyes fixated on Gaston's. He's watching her like a hungry wolf. I move my attention to the man opposite standing as best man. Taren. His eyes aren't fixed on the bride like everyone else's. They're fixed on me.

I tear my eyes from him, focusing on my best friend's wedding. Luna and Kali stand on either side of me. We're all Blake's bridesmaids, and she said she couldn't pick a maid of honor, so we all have to fulfill the role.

Luna subtly wipes a tear from her cheek as she watches. Kali smiles as she watches Blake get closer. We've had one crazy whirlwind of a year after surviving being kidnapped by the cartel.

Gaston, as he promised, followed Blake back to Brown and spent months stalking her like some psycho. And to all of our surprise, it worked. Blake fell for him of her own accord, and now they're getting married.

Since I graduated, Taren and I are living together in Boston. Kali and Luna got their own apartment in Boston, which Matias and Thiago have moved into. I'll never understand how Kali has fallen for Matias. All three of us can't understand it, as he's a true psychopath, and Kali is so sweet and innocent. It makes no logical sense. But she loves him.

It's amusing, or perhaps ironic, how our chaotic experience in Mexico plunged us into relationships with the men implicated in our capture. But then again, maybe we're all beautifully messed up in our own ways.

As Blake stands in front of Gaston, he takes her hands. A bloom of pink taints her cheeks just from how he looks at her. The officiant starts the ceremony and everyone is silent. Only the soft murmur of the ocean waves and the officiant's voice pierces the air.

After meeting and getting to know Gaston, I must admit they're meant for each other. They're both so similar in so many ways. I think it's why they clashed at the start, although Gaston just somehow knew they were meant for each other.

They begin to recite their vows. Gaston's voice undulates over the soft murmur of the ocean waves. He's oddly poetic for a man that comes off cold and calculated.

And then Blake says her vows. Her voice is soft and yet firm.

The sun begins its descent, setting just behind them, casting a warm, golden hue over the scene. The picturesque setting is like a beautifully painted canvas, with the ocean as its backdrop and two unlikely lovers pledging their eternal love as the centerpiece.

As the last word of Blake's vow fades away, a momentary silence descends over the crowd. Then, as if on cue, Gaston leans into Blake, their lips meeting in a soft, lingering kiss that seals their vows.

A cheer erupts from the crowd, a symphony of joyous whoops and applause that blends with the lapping waves. And as the sun dips below the horizon,

Gaston and Blake, hand in hand, turn to face their guests.

Then they walk back down the altar toward the huge gazebo set on the beach where the reception will be held.

Taren joins me, his hands slipping into mine as he maneuvers through the crowd. "I didn't like being apart from you," he breathes into my ear.

I shake my head. "Don't be silly. It wasn't for long."

He squeezes my hand. "Anytime apart is too long."

As we reach the gazebo, I look around at the fine details of the reception. Every table is meticulously decorated, shimmering under the warm glow of string lights that crisscross above us. With Gaston's wealth, it's no surprise he would go for such extravagance. But there's a touch of Blake, too - the rustic charm, the aromatic flowers, the understated elegance.

We sit at the main table where Gaston and Blake are sitting. Her parents don't approve of her match with Gaston despite his success. It turns out they're pretty racist and don't like foreigners. It's hard to believe they brought up Blake, one of the most open, inclusive people I know. They refused to attend the wedding, especially after Blake told them she wasn't taking the internship her dad secured for her and was moving to Mexico City. It's a shame they can't be happy for their daughter.

So, the bridal party is at their table rather than family. Matias and Kali are already in their seats. Matias has his arm around her shoulders possessively, and Kali blushes as he quietly says something.

"That was beautiful," I say, smiling at Blake as I sit beside her.

She turns to me and squeezes my hand. "I can't believe how happy I am."

I shake my head. "Neither can I, considering the two of you were at each other's throats just a few months ago."

Gaston clears his throat. "I was never at her throat. Blake is the one who enjoyed fighting me." He squeezes her hand. "I loved that fight. It's part of what I fell for."

He looks at her with such love. It's amazing.

"Careful, Marques, or people will think you actually have a heart," Taren teases.

Gaston glares at him. "No one would think that. My ruthlessness precedes me."

Thiago and Luna join us at the table, their hands entwined. Thiago pulls out the chair for Luna, and she smiles at him, a slight blush creeping up her cheeks. She seems to have found happiness with this man.

"Nice of you to finally join us," Taren mockingly says.

Luna flips him off, earning a chuckle from Thiago. "We were enjoying the sunset. Can't you lay off the sarcasm for once?"

Thiago raises an eyebrow in Taren's direction. "She has a point; it's a wedding, after all. Time for celebration, not banter."

"Alright, alright," Taren concedes, raising his hands. "I won't be the one to spoil the mood."

Clinking his glass against Matias', Gaston smirks. "Too late for that, I think. But let's make a toast for new beginnings and old friendships. To love in all its fucked up glory."

"To love!" we all chime in, raising our glasses. The night carries on, filled with laughter, shared stories, and the occasional tear. We're all a little fucked up, but maybe that's what makes this moment more beautiful.

As the night winds down, Taren leans toward me. "I want to show you something."

I frown at him, but don't argue as he grabs my hand and leads me out of the gazebo and away from the party.

"Where are we going?" I ask, staring at the dimly lit beach before us.

"Patience is a virtue, baby. Wait and see."

Taren's grip tightens around my hand as we veer off from the party's twinkling lights and into the darkness. A soft glow soon comes into view, casting long shadows over the sand and frothy waves. As we approach, the glow intensifies, revealing a small cove sheltered by towering cliffs.

In the middle, a blanket lies spread out, bordered by flickering candles that dance in the night breeze. Taren guides me toward the blanket, releasing my hand only to pick up a bottle of wine positioned conveniently beside a pair of empty glasses.

"What is all this?" I ask.

He ignores my question, pouring me a drink and handing it to me.

"Taren?" I push.

He smirks at me and I know he will just keep ignoring me.

"Patience is a virtue, right?"

He nods and doesn't pour himself a glass. Instead, he gets onto one knee. My heart rate quickens, and every muscle in my body tenses when he pulls out a small black box.

Opening the small black box, Taren reveals a dazzling ring that glitters under the moonlight. My breath hitches as he looks up at me, his eyes filled with a burning determination that has my heart pounding.

"From the moment I met you, I knew you were different. You're fierce, strong, and have a spirit that cannot be tamed," he begins. "You've seen me at my best and worst, yet you stood by me. Like calls to like, and you're my perfect match, Alice." He takes a deep breath, his eyes never leaving mine. "I want to spend the rest of my life with you. I want to wake up every morning knowing I'm yours and you are mine. I cannot promise a life without chaos, but I can promise to stand by you, no matter what. Will you marry me?"

So many emotions hit me all at once. I never saw myself agreeing to marriage, yet as I stare into Taren's dark eyes, I know I want to be with him forever. There is no world where I can survive without him. "Yes," I breathe.

He smiles a heart stopping smile and slips the ring onto my finger before standing. "Good, because I wouldn't have been pleased if you'd said no."

I arch a brow. "What would you have done?" I ask.

His smile widens. "I would have tortured you, edging you over and over until you finally agreed to marry me; otherwise, I wouldn't let you come."

I laugh. "You know how stubborn I am. I might have waited you out all night."

He leans toward my ear. "Shall we test how long you can last?" he murmurs. He pushes me back onto the soft blanket beneath us swiftly. The sensation of the cool sand beneath the thin fabric sends a thrill up my spine.

His gaze darkens, and I see the intent clear as day in the moon's dim light. He's in a playful mood, and I know I'm his favorite toy.

"Well, I must say," he murmurs, his lips brushing my ear, "I'm glad you've got no panties on, my dirty little bird." He slides his hand up my thigh, smirking. "It makes this much easier."

He slides a finger to my center and pushes it inside, making me moan. "I'm going to have a lot of fun with you." He curls his finger in the way he knows drives me crazy.

It's crazy how my desire for this man only grows. It knows no bounds. Taren adds another finger and curls them again, making me cry out. This man can play me like a fucking violin. "Please," I beg,

His smirk widens. "Didn't last long, did you? All I've done is finger you a bit, and you're already begging, little bird."

I bite my lip. "I need to come."

He chuckles. "I love how easy you are after a few drinks. But you won't be coming until my dick is inside you." He arches a brow. "Ass or pussy, your choice."

I'm about to speak when he cuts me off with his hand around my throat. "And it's the only choice you get tonight."

"Ass," I say.

He smirks. "Thought you'd say that. Lucky I've got some lube, isn't it?"

I moan as he flips me over roughly, and then I feel his tongue probing at my asshole. Ever since he suggested we try anal about six months ago, I've been obsessed. I can't get enough. He says he's going to work me up to double penetration. I say that it's impossible. There's no way he can fit a dildo in my pussy while he fucks my ass, but I think he took that as a challenge.

"Tonight is the night," he murmurs.

"The night for what?"

"For you to take my dick and this dildo," he says as if he read my fucking mind. And then he slams the dildo inside my pussy, making me moan.

I moan, the idea arousing but the uncertainty of it being possible clawing at my mind. "You know I can't fit that and you inside me simultaneously."

"I beg to differ," he replies.

"Relax, little bird," Taren murmurs.

I can feel his fingers at my entrance, his touch cool and teasing as he works lube into my tight hole. The pressure builds as he stretches me, first with one finger, then two, his movements slow and deliberate. He doesn't stop until he's got all four fingers stretching me.

I groan, the mix of pleasure and discomfort making me clench around the dildo still inside me. Not missing a beat, he replaces his fingers with a large butt plug, pushing it gently into place.

"Oh my God," I breathe, shocked at how good it feels to be so full.

"You like that, don't you?" Taren whispers, his voice rough and filled with desire. "You're so full, aren't you, little bird? I've got you stretched just right. Can you take more?"

The idea of him, of the fullness and the intensity, is both terrifying and tantalizing. "I don't think so."

He chuckles. "Let's find out."

He pulls the butt plug from my ass, and then I feel him pouring more cold lube into and around my stretched hole.

"Taren, wait..." I manage to gasp out as he lines his huge cock up with my hole.

"That's not the word to stop this, little bird."

I know it's not. And deep down, I don't want to stop it.

"No, don't do this," I add.

He chuckles and pushes forward, his cock stretching my tight hole. I scream in both pleasure and pain as he stretches me in a way I've never been stretched before. My pussy is throbbing as I feel his cock pressing against the dildo.

"Good girl," he murmurs. "You're doing so fucking well, Alice. Taking my cock in your ass and a dildo in your pussy." He's slow but forceful as he keeps moving until every inch of his dick is buried in my ass.

"Fuck," I breathe.

"How does it feel, little bird? Are you stuffed full?"

I nod in response, knowing I can't find my voice right now even if I wanted to.

Taren starts to move, his cock sliding smoothly in and out of my ass, the dildo still filling my pussy. The sensation is overwhelming, pleasure and discomfort mingling in intense waves.

I feel my muscles gradually relax, accepting this new level of fullness. And I can't believe that the raw intensity of the double penetration becomes something I crave more of. "Fuck, Taren," I moan, the words torn from me as the rhythm of his movements increases.

His cock moves against the dildo inside me, pleasure and desire pulsing through every nerve. My mind is a whirl of ecstasy, the dual pleasure of the dildo and

Taren's cock sending me spiraling toward an orgasm I can feel building deep within. "Oh God, Taren... it's... it's so good," I pant, the words barely a whisper. "I'm going to—"

He freezes and grabs my throat, cutting my oxygen off. "No, you're not coming yet. You come when I say, and I haven't had enough of fucking this tight little ass while your pussy is stuffed so full. It's heaven, and I want this to last all night."

I whimper. "Then make me come repeatedly," I breathe.

He chuckles. "Greedy, aren't you?"

I groan in response, knowing he's going to torture me.

"Problem is your ass feels too fucking good, and the moment you come, then you'll milk my dick with your tight fucking ass."

"Good," I breathe. "I want you to fill my ass with cum all night," I goad, knowing what drives him wild.

"Fuck," he growls. "Naughty Alice is trying to goad me into fucking her hard, isn't she?"

With an animalistic growl, Taren gives in to his primal desires and plunges into me with abandon. His control shatters as he chases our shared release, the brutal rhythm of his movements pushing us both to the edge.

I feel him throb inside me, his cock swells, and I know he's close. "Come for me, Alice," he gasps, the command simultaneously a plea. With a cry, I shatter, my orgasm ripping through me. A moment later, Taren's own climax hits him, hot and potent. His cum fills my ass, his roar of satisfaction mingling with my own cries. It's raw, it's dirty, it's perfect. And it's just the beginning of a very long fucking night.

He collapses onto the blanket, leaving the dildo in my pussy. And then he yanks me against him, breathing raggedly. "I'm going to do that so many times tonight you literally will be leaking cum from your ass all week," he promises.

I glance up at him and smile. "Good."

He growls. "So dirty, aren't you?"

"Yeah, and you love it."

He nods. "I love you, little bird. Forever and always. Until the sun no longer shines in the fucking sky. I'll love you with all my heart."

I kiss him softly. "I love you too. My mad hatter."

He chuckles against my lips. "My little bird."

As I lay nestled in Taren's arms, the heat of our bodies cooling after the passionate frenzy, I can't help but reflect on our journey from me being a cage in the basement of the Navarro Cartel mansion to the fiancé of the new boss of the Navarro Cartel. It's an insane change, but one that makes perfect sense. My darker corners fit perfectly into Taren's jagged edges and vice versa. We're survivors, warriors who battle our demons and find peace in the love we share. And I wouldn't change one thing about how our meeting played out. It's twisted and dark, but it's our story to cherish. Forever and always.

THANK you so much for reading Unhinged. I hope you enjoyed following Alice & Taren's story. Going forward, I'm going to be working a little differently with my releases and schedule.

I've had some health issues this year and found time constraints difficult. Therefore, I've decided that instead of putting books on pre-order, for the moment I'll just announce releases on social media and through my newsletter and release them immediately once they're ready. It'll ensure I don't have to delay new releases but also don't have the pressure of deadlines to work with. So, while I've got the cover reveal and blurb below for the next book, there's no release date yet.

This should help speed up my releases, as it can sometimes stifle creativity working under a deadline!

I wish you all a happy and healthy new year.

The next book will follow Alice's friend, Blake, after Gaston purchased her from the Navarro Cartel.

Beast: A Dark Billionaire Romance

I'M JUST a pawn in a game for Mexico's wealthiest, cruelest man.

Following my abduction, I find myself in the opulent home of Gaston Marques, Mexico's most feared billionaire. He's dark, he's dangerous, and he's obsessed with possessing me. I detest him and resist him, but he doesn't care. He takes what he wants, and he wants me.

But then, something shifts. In this gilded cage, I see glimpses of a different side of Gaston amidst the darkness. And against all my better judgment, I find myself drawn to him, pulled in by his magnetism. Even as I push back, I can't deny his strange and powerful attraction.

When my friends devise a daring plan to rescue me, Gaston lets me go. But there's a twist. He follows me. He's determined to win me over in my world, a place where he's the outsider, not me. I tell him it's impossible, that we could never be. But love, especially one as twisted and intoxicating as ours, doesn't play by the rules.

Beast is the fifth book in the Once Upon a Villain Series by Bianca Cole. This dark, billionaire mafia romance explores themes that may be disturbing to some readers. No cliffhanger and a happily-ever-after ending means this book can be read as a standalone.

Dirty Secret: A Dark Enemies to Loves Mafia Romance

Dark Crown: A Dark Arranged Marriage Romance

Boston Mafia Dons Series

Empire of Carnage: A Dark Captive Mafia Romance

Cruel Daddy: A Dark Mafia Arranged Marriage Romance

Savage Daddy: A Dark Captive Mafia Romance

Ruthless Daddy: A Dark Forbidden Mafia Romance

Vicious Daddy: A Dark Brother's Best Friend Mafia Romance

Wicked Daddy: A Dark Captive Mafia Romance

New York Mafia DonsSeries

Her Irish Daddy: A Dark Mafia Romance

Her Russian Daddy: A Dark Mafia Romance

Her Italian Daddy: A Dark Mafia Romance

Her Cartel Daddy: A Dark Mafia Romance

Romano Mafia Brother's Series

Her Mafia Daddy: A Dark Daddy Romance

Her Mafia Boss: A Dark Romance

Her Mafia King: A Dark Romance

New York Brotherhood Series

Bought: A Dark Mafia Romance

Captured: A Dark Mafia Romance

Claimed: A Dark Mafia Romance

Bound: A Dark Mafia Romance

Taken: A Dark Mafia Romance

Forbidden Desires Series

Bryson: An Enemies to Lovers Office Romance

Logan: A First Time Professor And Student Romance

Ryder: An Enemies to Lovers Office Romance

Dr. Fox: A Forbidden Romance

Royally Mated Series

Her Faerie King: A Faerie Royalty Paranormal Romance

Her Alpha King: A Royal Wolf Shifter Paranormal Romance

Her Dragon King: A Dragon Shifter Paranormal Romance

Her Vampire King: A Dark Vampire Romance

ABOUT THE AUTHOR

I love to write stories about over the top alpha bad boys who have heart beneath it all, fiery heroines, and happily-ever-after endings with heart and heat. My stories have twists and turns that will keep you flipping the pages and heat to set your kindle on fire.

For as long as I can remember, I've been a sucker for a good romance story. I've always loved to read. Suddenly, I realized why not combine my love of two things, books and romance?

My love of writing has grown over the past four years and I now publish on Amazon exclusively, weaving stories about dirty mafia bad boys and the women they fall head over heels in love with.

If you enjoyed this book please follow me on Amazon, Bookbub or any of the below social media platforms for alerts when more books are released.

Printed in Great Britain
by Amazon

36241772R00209